Sci·fi & fantasy
modeller

volume 39

Sci·fi & fantasy modeller

Editor-in-Chief/co-Publisher: *Michael G. Reccia.*
Specials Editor: *Andy Pearson.*
Art Editor/co-Publisher: *David Openshaw.*
Regular modelling team: *Iain Costall, Jim Costello, Barry Ford, Jason C. Gares, Andy Pearson, Gary R. Welsh.*
This volume's contributors: *Roberto Aguilera, Diego Cuenca, Steve Howarth, Senthil Nathan, Bob Smith.*

web: *www.scififantasymodeller.co.uk*
editorial email: *info@scififantasymodeller.co.uk*
Published by Happy Medium Press copyright © 2015
ISBN-13: 978-0-9930320-3-5
Printed in the United Kingdom by Pioneer Print Solutions.

VOLUME 39 EDITORIAL

Moving Pictures

This issue I'm delighted to announce that Jason C. Gares has joined our regular modelling and writing team. Genre modellers who read each and every volume of this title (*is there any other kind*, I ask myself sagely) will already be familiar with Jason's work as he has entertained us with some fascinating and informative articles over our last couple of issues – and serial visitors to our website (*is there any other kind*, I ask myself hypothetically) will also know that Jason is entertaining us regularly there too, courtesy of a monthly blog that includes a video on his chosen subject. So far he's built and reviewed *Bandai*'s *Star Wars Stormtrooper* kit and has delivered the initial entry in a series looking at and customising *DeAgostini*'s huge *Milennium Falcon* partwork kit, which I'm sure many of you are currently building (I know I am – I want all the parts now. *Now, I tell you!*). Welcome to the team, Jason.

On the subject of blogs, hallowed teamster Gary Welsh also has a couple of sparkling new entries for you to read on site, so why not make a visit to scififantasymodeller.co.uk a regular occurence at least once a month? It will help ease the wait between Volumes of *Sci-fi & fantasy modeller*. ...You never know, I might even find the time to add much-promised new entries to my blog page every now and again should time and circumstances allow.

What the...?

What's that noise?

...Damn pigs – they keep dive-bombing the windows!

Take care, thank you for reading, and see you in ninety.

Michael G. Reccia
Editor-In-Chief

 Follow us on Facebook [http://www.facebook.com/pages/Scifi-fantasy-modeller/110020029085161] and Twitter [http://twitter.com/#!/SffModeller].

ROUND 2

The WIZARD of Oz
WICKED WITCH OF THE WEST

RESIN FIGURE MODEL KIT • SKILL LEVEL 3 • AGES 12+   POLAR LIGHTS

Jamie Hood of *Round 2* reports:

King Kong and the Wicked Witch (box art above) – kits are on track for release in the Nov/Dec timeframe.

U.S.S. Enterprise; Klingon Battle Cruiser, Ships of the Line kits – the images show our packages for the

preprinted kits and a closer look at some of the trading cards, produced by *Rittenhouse Archives*, that are included in the *SotL* series.

U.S.S. Excelsior – this is still under construction and we are at the digital mockup stage with the factory. Once we get to the point of the physical mockup, I'll start sharing more on that. It is getting a little late to

say the kit will release this year – so more likely to be early in 2016.

Headless Horseman – the kit will be reissued in the fourth quarter of 2015 with new packaging.

1989 Batman Batwing – we will be bringing this kit back out in early 2016. We'll include a dome base and the packaging will be all new along the lines of the *Batmobile* kit that should be available by the time you read this. (Pictured *Batwing* buildup by Jim Small.)

1/48th. Space 1999 Eagle – see our special progress report this issue – Ed.

Headless Horseman

THE WEATHERING MAGAZINE

The world's only modelling magazine devoted entirely to painting and creating weathering effects. The title explains, via detailed step by step articles, various techniques from some of the world's top modellers. SF and fantasy subjects are included, and the methods illustrated apply to all aspects of the modelling hobby. The current issue includes a highly detailed 'J-style' steampunk-esque diorama with figures and fantasy walker vehicle.

IN COMBAT – PAINTING MECHAS

For decades robots and other massive SF war machines have been amongst the most popular subjects modelled throughout Asia and the rest of the world. *Bandai* popularised this fascinating aspect of our hobby with the *Gundams* made and collected today by many genre modellers. This new book offers *Mecha* lovers unique, highly realistic new ways to paint, weather, convert and finish their kits in detailed articles packed with techniques and tips. A beautifully presented 92-page colour paperback.

WASHES AND PIGMENTS

A comprehensive selection of *MIG* detailing and weathering washes and pigments was received recently for inclusion in *HFTM*. These have us salivating uncontrollably here and will be of great interest to the serious SF modeller. They range from *Light Dust* to *Gun Metal* and various *Rust* shades in pigment form to enamel washes offering such specific finishes as *Fresh Engine Oil* and *Fuel Stains* to *Streaking Grime*. Also available are themed paint packs such as *Rust Effects Colours*, containing six acrylic rust tone paints for airbrush use, and *Mechas and Robots Colours*, featuring six specialist acrylics suitable for airbrush and brush.

Full details:
www.ammomigjimenez-usa.com / *migjimenez.com*

PARAGRAFIX

FALCON COCKPIT SET FOR DEAGOSTINI KIT ISSUES 1–7

The first in a series of accurising, superdetail upgrades for the *DeAgostini Millennium Falcon* partwork kit is available now from *Paragrafix* [1]. The cockpit set features replacement rear bulkhead, main controls, flight console and even tiny bonus headsets! A comprehensive decal set is also provided. MSRP $59.95.

A second set is in production [2-3] for release shortly, and this will enable modellers to superdetail the main hold, via an exact pattern floor, down to the number of grid patterns in each section. The two maintenance hatchways can be removed and there are brackets to mount the I-beams that are sometimes in place. The floor can be installed without modification of the kit part – if the maintenance hatchways are to be displayed open, then some surgery will be required to remove the area underneath them. Also included will be the control panels behind the seating, as well as the small panel at the end of the banquette.

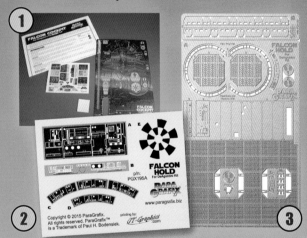

CLASSIC THUNDERBIRDS

NEW EPISODES IN PRE-PRODUCTION

50 YEARS AFTER THUNDERBIRDS HIT OUR SCREENS, THE ICONIC PUPPETS WILL RETURN IN BRAND NEW EPISODES thanks to **Thunderbirds 1965**, a project by director Stephen La Rivière, supported by the Gerry Anderson estate, Sylvia Anderson, and ITV.

In addition to the series, three audio episodes were launched in 1966, with music and dialogue from the original voice cast. **Thunderbirds 1965** will see La Rivière film the **Thunderbirds** puppets and sets he recreated for 2014's **Filmed in Supermarionation** documentary using classic *Supermarionation* techniques, and combine this with the audio recordings to create three new episodes.

Thunderbirds 1965 launched on *Kickstarter* July 9th and has far exceeded its £75,000 base goal, reaching *Kickstarter*'s current list of most popular projects.

Backing the project is the only way fans can watch the episodes. In addition to a DVD/Blu-ray of the finished production, backers have the opportunity to receive other rewards including a commemorative photo-book featuring previously unpublished stills from the series and an exclusive 'Thunderbirds Experience' giving them the chance to visit the studio and experience first-hand the model and puppet filmmaking techniques first developed fifty years ago. The recreated stars will also be around for meet and greets.

The campaign aims to raise £120,000 to fund two of three special episodes. If the project surpasses this 'stretch goal' a further goal to enable production of episode three will be introduced.

Thunderbirds 1965 will be produced by the team behind *Filmed in Supermarionation*, which tells the story of the pioneering production of **Thunderbirds**, **Stingray**, **Captain Scarlet**, etc.

Jamie Anderson, son of Gerry says: 'Generations have enjoyed **Thunderbirds**. The magic formula of models, practical effects and puppets is very special, and I'm certain Stephen and his team will recreate that magic.'

Stephen La Rivière: 'For *Filmed In Supermarionation* we shot new sequences with puppets using the old techniques. Whilst the methods seem a little archaic and time-consuming by today's standards, we thought it would be very special to do a one-off project bringing **Thunderbirds** back to life 1960s style. Sadly, many of the original cast have passed away since 1965. However, thanks to these recordings, we have new stories that have never been adapted for screen. This means these old-new episodes should be the most authentic recreation of the 1960s' experience it's possible to get.'

continued page 82!

Team Cloud Car

Roberto Aguilera and friends build a Studio Scale Star Wars replica

Two years ago I re-opened the box containing a very unusual **Star Wars** vehicle I'd bought on *eBay* in 2007. It was time to give birth to this studio scale *Bespin Cloud Car* that, after some research, I'd discovered was a kit made by Tobias Robum in 1/9 scale, which was probably limited to fifty or so copies.

The *Car* had been very poorly cast, with lots of bubbles in the resin. The cockpits were badly cast too, and rather thick, and there was pretty much no interior to speak off and no pilots either, the interior of the *Pods* being completely filled with foam. Additionally some of the parts were missing! The amount of work needed was overwhelming but as this was the only kit of the subject available I decided to ask for some help from my friends so that the *Cloud Car* could see the light of day.

The build

Analysing the kit, there were things that needed to be done initially before we could begin construction: the model somehow had to be corrected in shape, and it also had a bent engine piece – a block of resin that could in no way be straightened.

I called my friend Gerardo Cortes ('the Human') who is very good at these types of build challenges. He took the model away with him and began heating it and coaxing it back into shape, inserting two substantial metal tubes across the vehicle to align the *Pods* and the engine.

Geraldo carved out pretty much all of the foam from inside the *Pods* so that the cockpits could be fitted in, and began filling some of the major holes caused by air bubbles. We also cast four 1/35

Humvee engines to place behind the vents on the lower end section of the *Pods* so you could look through the vents and discover something behind them.

Lighting was obviously something I wanted to feature in a vehicle of this scale, and my friend Hector Humen, a specialist in this area, provided the LED lighting for the engines and cockpits. He cast the back engine piece too, building the lighting tubes and fitting them perfectly. *Rosco Film Light Filters* were added to the LED lights in the engine to provide the correct bluish colour and temperature.

As stated above, some parts were missing from the kit, and so, following some research and with a little help from my friends the right pictures and references were found. We needed a *Tamiya 1/12 Martini Brabham F1* for the mount on the guns and some extra details around the cockpit, so a kit was duly ordered. I have to say that it was a very pleasant experience to open the kit box and find not only the parts for this project but also many more **Star Wars** kit-bash pieces inside…

Cockpits and Pilots

At this stage we had to tackle a major aspect of our 'to do' list… the original cockpit cages were really bad castings so they needed to be rebuilt from scratch. My friend Alberto Barba, who is a great modeller and an accomplished scratchbuilder, was next to take the model away, and he began to create the cages for the cockpits from styrene sheet. He also straightened the engine piece and gave me a hand in filling in many of the bubbles on the kit's surface. Long time buddy Rafael Romo then took the *Pods* and began a major part of the build for the model – the cockpits and pilots.

I found a couple of 1/9 aeroplane RC pilots on *eBay*. The pilot figures were suitable for the project although there was nothing special about them with the exception of their faces, which were really well sculpted.

Undertaking some research Rafael found some pictures of the original figures from the studio miniature, which we used as reference only as they were too basic and non realistic. We wanted the real thing… realistic-looking pilots.

Roberto at work on the *Cloud Car.*

Scratchbuilt cockpit tub.

Test-fitting tub into *Car.*

Primed cockpit tub.

Seats are added to the tub assembly.

Positioning figures.

One of the completed tubs in *Cloud Car Pod*.

Rough cockpit canopy test-fitted on one of the *Pods*. Roof window has yet to be cut away.

The figures were thinned down with a motor tool and sanding and *Magic Sculpt* was layered on carefully to sculpt the clothing. The faces were left untouched, with the exception of the co-pilot's *Magic Sculpt* moustache.

The helmets were created with two-part epoxy putty and sanded; the stripes on the helmets were moulded with styrene strip, and the remaining helmet details were made with a punch-die set. Belt buckles were fashioned from bare metal foil, and guns, holsters and belt pouches were also included.

I added the glasses after painting, with two little pieces of *Rosco Film Lighting Filter ND6*, hand cutting them with scissors and placing them in position.

As Rafael was attempting to fix the pilots in situ he realised their shoulders were not fitting in properly, and that the figures needed to be positioned lower than we had first thought, meaning the cockpits would need to be bigger and more detailed.

We had never liked the original *ILM* cockpit or figures, so we just took those as a reference and a starting point. We began to re-invent how the cockpit should look (on the original model it is just a black, square box with a seat and no detail).

The basic shape of the cockpit was created from styrene and a lot of kit-bashing, using a variety of subjects from **Star Trek** to **Star Wars** (including the *MPC speeder bike*) and the seats were sculpted from putty and detailed with some kit parts. Rafael had the idea of using **Star Wars** kits as part of the bashing, bringing the model closer to the **SW** universe, a move which I totally agreed with. Not much of the cockpits can be seen now, and we knew this would be the case, but the detailing gives the feel that everything is in there.

Dashboards were also a major detail, as they were going to be seen a lot and from every angle. The frames were made from styrene, and my friend Marco Antonio Ortiz, who is a designer, created the acetates for the dashboards using some Ralph McQuarrie artwork paintings. Once the acetates were finished and place, fibre optics were added.

Lighting in scale is a very delicate operation as the scale itself dictates the intensity of the light source – many lit scale models are too bright, the light scale makes no sense, and a dimmer should have been added to regulate the intensity.

With all rectifications, alterations and building complete, the kit was finally put together, with us adding final details, screws, and the two rectangular metal foil panels below the car.

At this point a major build issue needed to be addressed... I had to paint the pilots and the cockpits, connect the dashboards and close the *Cloud Car*. I needed to do a lot of masking while painting this kit, and, once assembled, I would not be able to manipulate such a large model. Further, with the pilots in place, I could not place it upside down. I decided to paint the body first, to close the *Pods* later, and to add the styrene strip in the middle gap after painting, which was not going to be easy.

Painting

The entire concept of painting the *Cloud Car* was fascinating, taking in the music of *Bespin* and Ralph McQuarrie's concept art along the way. I just went crazy about it, researching all the shots of the models I could find on the internet, plus all available colour pictures and books so that I could study all possible oranges and browns for the paint finish.

I found some pictures of the *ESB* studio scale *Cloud Car* at an exhibition, these having been taken at the perfect distance from the model with a flash. The colour reproduction was very accurate and you could see the panels and markings on the *Car*. The colour is actually a bright red-orange, and that made perfect sense to me right away... on screen you see a dull orange/brown ship, reproduced in most **SW** toys such as those released by *Kenner/Hasbro*. The ship was lit by *ILM* using a *Lee Filters 286 Burnt Yellow* on the lights. For the shoot the exposure was set to the key light to show the ship in a sunset, resulting in high contrast shots. Also remember that the model shots were composites, meaning that, in order to see that much colour on screen you had go with even more vibrant colours on the actual model. The pictures from the exhibition revealed a bright orange, with a variation of this colour on some of the panels. Certain panels are darker – almost red in colour, while some are a lighter beige/orange –

Cleaned up canopy with roof window opened up.

1/9th scale RC pilots were thinned down with a motor tool and *Magic Sculpt* was then applied to create their clothing.

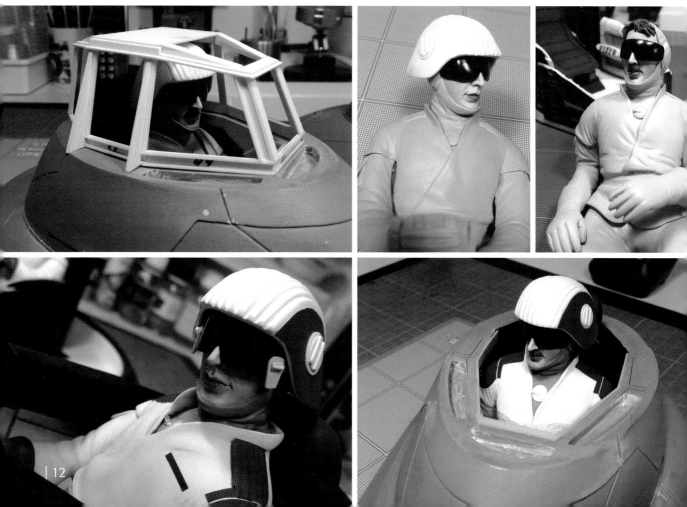

One of the completed figures wearing visor created from *Rosco Film Lighting Filter ND6.*

Pilot test-fitted into one of the *Pods* to determine correct height and attitude within the cockpit canopy.

Final canopy detailing added prior to priming.

almost a flesh tone. The violet red also came from studying the reference pictures, from which I deduced that the cockpits seem to have black seats and interiors, with the interior frames also having been painted black.

Painting and finishing the pilots

I've seen reference pictures of the original *ILM* figures, which in my opinion have a slight off-white creamy tone – almost a white-cream – to their clothing... I love the idea of the elegant *Bespin* city reflected in colour tone in its buildings and inhabitants. Shadows on the clothing were created by airbrushing on *Lifecolor Portland Stone UA 107.*

The red on the helmets and clothing was *Vallejo Cavalry Red* painted on straight from the bottle. With everything masked and airbrushed, a coat of satin gloss/varnish was applied to the helmets, and decals supplied from a 1/48 scale *Hellcat* were placed on the side of the chests.

The faces were airbrushed in *Tamiya Flesh* and, after further detail had been added with a *Lifecolor Flesh Set*, hand painted shadows and lights were applied, slightly washed with *Winsor*

& Newton Raw Umber oil. On a 1/9 scale figure painting needs to be subtle due to the larger scale.

As stated, the interiors of the cockpits were, according to reference, simply black, so I decided to add some depth to the model by adding more interesting colours to the basic *Bespin* palette. I painted in the dashboard frames and outer rims of the cockpits with a mix of *Vallejo Black* and *German Cam Black Brown 70979*; the lower sections of the cockpits were painted *Vallejo Pale Sand 70837* as I wanted a lighter colour underneath, and *MIG Neutral* oil washes were applied to the lower sections. The seats were airbrushed with *Lifecolor Worn Black UA 734,* and shadows airbrushed with *Lifecolor Black.*

The Pods

The first thing was to achieve a real chipped paint effect on this large scale model, and I therefore needed an acrylic paint that could be mixed in large bottles with a full range of combinations, and that was soft enough to chip, yet tough enough to achieve the desired thickness. I picked *Vallejo Model Color* for this. A mix of *Bright Orange 70851, Orange Red 70910, Flat Red 70957, Deep Yellow 70915* and *Tan Yellow 912*

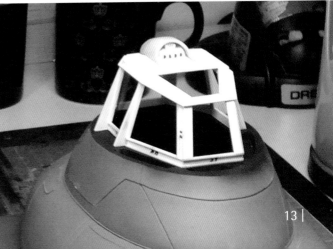

formed the base mix colour of the *Cloud Car*, the tan variation being created by adding 50 percent of *German Orange 70911* and *Light Orange 70911* to the base mix. The Darker variation was mixed by adding 50 percent of *Red 70926* to the base mix.

Panels on the sides of the cockpits, as well as the tubing on the engine, were painted with a mix of *Vallejo Dark Red 946*, *Purple 70959* and *Violet Red 70812*. I primed the *Pods'* upper and lower sections and the cockpits with *Tamiya Fine White Primer* – around ten coats were applied to soften the surface and smooth tiny bubbles.

I always apply an enamel strong base coat when chipping is to be carried out, so the model was sprayed using *Tamiya TS 83 Metallic Silver* in a couple of thin coats which I let dry for two days.

After this my life turned into one long masking tape exercise, with me masking each panel and covering the rest to prevent the intrusion of paint into areas where I didn't want it to go. Each panel was individually masked then airbrushed with *AK Worn Effects Fluid*, allowing this to dry for about

twenty minutes then airbrushing thin coats of the mix to achieve a balance between thickness and chipping. Also the intensity of the colour is based on the number of layers applied – I airbrushed around seven layers of the mix on per panel. Once the paint had dried for a day I removed the masking and began 'chipping' with a thin brush, applying water with a brush and gently rubbing the paint on the edges of the panels. I also added some scratches to the surface, all the while trying to achieve a correct sense of scale with the chipping.

With all chipping completed, I remasked each panel individually again so that I could apply shadows and flight burns with an airbrushed dark brown colour. I used *Vallejo Dark Brown* with the darker mix super-thinned down to produce a subtle effect as this is not a spaceship but a car.

As I wanted to achieve a worn look on the inside of the engine the intake was painted in *Tamiya TS 83 Metallic Silver*, which was then chipped before adding a thin layer of *Lifecolor Matt Black* over it, followed by heavy washes of *AK Light Rust* and MIG *Neutral Wash*. The markings on the *Pods* were masked and airbrushed with *Vallejo Leather Brown 70871*.

Test-fitting primed canopies and completed pilots.

Engine block rigged for lighting is connected to the *Pod* lower halves.

Primed *Pods* and Engine block.

Sub-assemblies completed.

Testing the lighting prior to painting.

Layering the various shades over a base coat of *Tamiya TS 83 Metallic Silver.*

Once the acrylic weathering process had been completed the *Car* was airbrushed with *Vallejo Satin Varnish,* three or four coats being applied to even out the look of the paint. After masking the *Violet Red* areas, the *Car* was then airbrushed with a thin coat of *AK Light Rust Wash,* letting that coat settle on the model for some days. This wash helped the original *Metallic Silver* underneath the base colour to appear yellowish, like a soft rust.

My next move was to airbrush a thin overall layer of super-thinned *AK Dark Brown Wash,* the panel lines and some weathering touches being painted with *Winsor & Newton Raw Umber* oil.

Final construction was very difficult as, with the sub-assemblies already painted, assembly was delicate and I had to avoid touching the *Car* as much as I possibly could. The cockpits were glued in place, the lights were connected and the *Pods* were closed using a great idea from my friend Gerardo Cortes, mentioned here because I was asked about this on a forum a few months ago and didn't get the chance to reply:

Six holes were drilled into the interior of the lower section of the *Pods.* We then placed six metal rods into these facing upwards, trimming them to the correct height of the upper *Pods* once they were in position. We then made six balls of epoxy putty and just pressed the *Pods* down onto the rods – a perfect, easy solution.

The outer middle strip was then added, painted and weathered using the same process chosen for the rest of the *Car.* The stand was painted with *Rosco Video Paint Blue Screen.* I love painting the stands with the actual paint used by the studio... it makes a model look 'ready to shoot'.

The model was finished ready for the October *IMPS* show in Mexico City, and our team of modellers were in attendance, all happy to share and see it finally finished, and agreeing that it was worth all the work to see such a unique piece of **Star Wars** history right in front of our eyes.

Special thanks to Daniel Perez Ares for the photographs and *Photoshop* work, and thank you all for reading. Let's keep sharing and building!

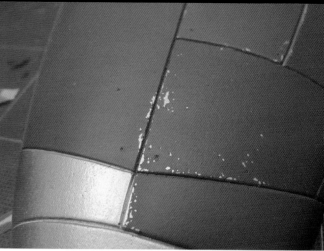

Oranges are chipped away to reveal the underlying silver to create a super-realistic weathering effect.

Completed *Cloud Car* features no glazing as per the original filming miniature.

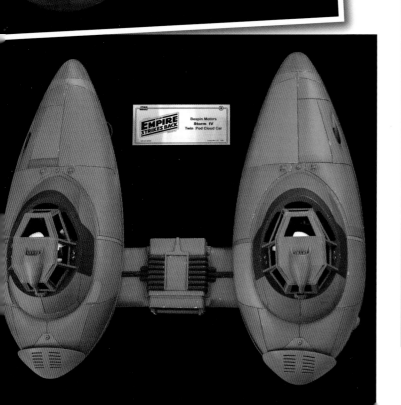

STAR WARS
EMPIRE
STRIKES BACK

Bespin Motors
Storm IV
Twin Pod Cloud Car

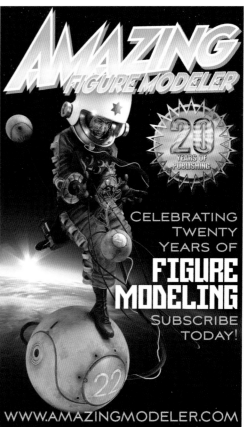

PROMETHEUS WAS THE LONG-AWAITED FILM FROM DIRECTOR RIDLEY SCOTT THAT WAS SPOKEN OF AS A FIFTH SEQUEL/INSTALLMENT IN THE **ALIEN** UNIVERSE, which he introduced us to in 1979. The story ended up not being directly connected to the **ALIEN** movies and, according to Scott, although the film shares 'strands of **ALIEN**'s DNA, so to speak', and takes place in the same universe, **Prometheus** explores its own mythology and ideas. Having the film share the same universe with, but not continue, the **ALIEN** storyline didn't sit well with many fans. In my opinion, even though changes were made to the look and feel of the film (making it stand alone from all other **ALIEN** movies), I believe Scott gave the world another great looking, exciting feature, even without true xenomorph creatures being present.

Freelance artist and sculptor Apikitt L. Highway took inspiration from **Prometheus** and sculpted, by hand and in clay, a 10½" bust of the *Engineer* featured in the movie. Apikitt worked for several months from many points of reference, including pictures from magazines, the internet and screen captures to get the proportions and details as close to the movie's *Engineer* as he could. Three points of interest he included in the final sculpt: a removable helmet revealing the head underneath; well detailed 'oozing' cannisters and the inclusion of the Alien wall reference as the main focal point of the base. (1–4) I contacted Apikitt after hearing of his project and found he was producing a limited run of this sculpt as a hollow resin model kit... without hesitation I ordered one.

The long journey of the *Engineer* bust from Thailand ended at my front door. On my studio workbench I cut the tape securing the box and unwrapped all the parts – the packaging of this kit was more impressive than what many companies with larger budgets provide. (5) I carefully inspected 12 resin parts: hollow body, head, helmet, 2 small hoses, 2 large hoses, helmet hose and 4 cannisters with 'ooze'. The resin this kit is made of is really light, but also brittle, so extra care needed to be taken when working on it. Overall, the parts were well detailed with little to no seam lines. Most astonishing was how well the

ON THE OUTER REACHES...

A study of the Engineer from Prometheus
Jason C. Gares

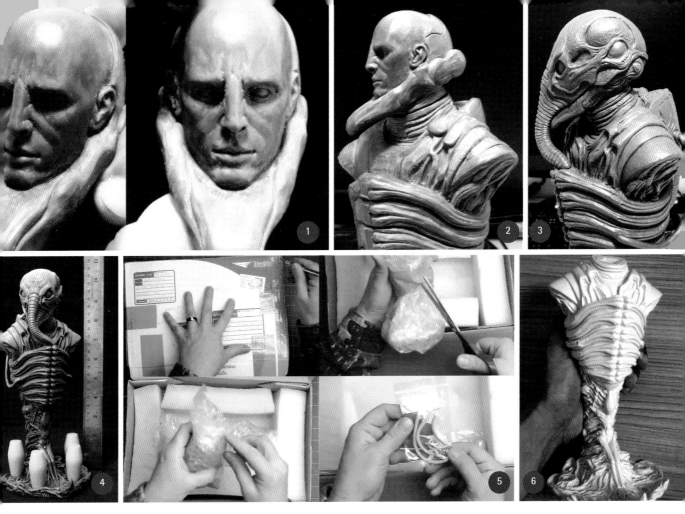

design of the helmet had been thought out, and how well it fit over the head, with more than enough clearance so the inside of the helmet wouldn't rub against the head after painting. (6–7) After a final check that everything was accounted for and intact, I washed the parts in hot water and dish soap, then let dry overnight.

Next day I drilled a small hole in the bottom of the head, in the centre of the neck, added 2-part, 5-minute epoxy inside the hole and inserted a small length of wire coat hanger to be used as a pin. I drilled the same size hole in the top-centre of the body, between the shoulders, also adding 2-part epoxy there. The head was inserted between the shoulders and left to harden overnight. I made sure to overfill the hole in the body so the epoxy would be squeezed out between the seam lines that lay between the upper part of the neck and lower part of the head and I wouldn't have to fill the small gap with putty. All I needed to do was use my motor tool to grind it down plus a dental tool to even out detail where the two connected. Again, using 2-part epoxy, I attached the two large hoses, one each side of the body, and the two small hoses between the right shoulder and neck, making sure they just touched the helmet when placed over the

head. Holes were drilled into both the front hose section of the helmet and the top of the curved hose that connects to it. A hanger rod was epoxied in place to connect the two and a little sanding done to hide the seam. Holes were drilled into the bottom of all four cannisters so rods could be inserted for holding during painting. With all prep work finished, it was time for painting.

The biggest, most challenging aspect of this resin bust wasn't building it, but painting it. Over my years of building and painting figures, the one big thing I've noticed is that building a figure really takes a backseat to the paint job that's applied. I'd go so far as to say accuracy even joins the building aspect in taking that back seat to the overall paint job. I'm not saying building and accuracy aren't as important – they are. But, if you aspire to have a figure build in a competition, be prepared to have your paint job scrutinised by the judges – painting is that important. It's the one part of the hobby that's looked at more as an art form than any other. Bearing this in mind I decided to go down an original path with the paint job as opposed to what was seen in the film. Since the *Engineers* are from deep space, I wanted this environmental suit to reflect that. I thought outside the box and

decided I wanted the suit to look like it was, as American astronomer Carl Sagan described us and the cosmos, 'made of star stuff'. I wanted to show stars, cosmic gas and different shades of light as part of the suit and had an idea of how I was going to achieve this. In short, most of the bust was going to end up looking close to that of a beetle's shell – a different approach to the film, and against what is considered 'cannon'…

As the bust was resin, I sprayed on three thin coats of *Krylon Gray Primer*. If I'd missed any seam lines or glued areas that needed sanding or filling the first time, I'd be able to see them a lot better now and take care of them before moving on. Once all my issues were finalised, I sprayed on two more coats of primer and let set for a couple of days. The next step was to apply several thin layers of *Createx Wicked Colors Wicked Black* with my *Sparmax HB-040* airbrush. After a few days drying I airbrushed *Testors Model Master Silver Chrome* over it, again in several light layers. (8) While the chrome was drying I picked out the colours I wanted to use for the 'star stuff' effect: *ComArt Transparent Ultramarine*, *Transparent Cadmium Yellow* and *Transparent Kelly Green*. The base colour for the head would be *ComArt*

Opaque White. (9)

I felt the layering of the colours should be carefully planned. As with past builds, I used a piece of plastic sheet and did some tests regarding my approach to the layering. It's always a good idea to test your paint and experiment on a scrap sheet of plastic so your actual subject doesn't get messed up. Also, I was using *ComArt* water-based paint over enamel, which meant, if I didn't like how things were going, I could wipe the paint away. Using my airbrush, I applied several coats of *ComArt Transparent Cadmium Yellow* in sections on the suit and helmet. This takes more passes than usual due to how transparent this colour is. The next couple of steps were applying *ComArt Transparent Ultramarine* next to the *Cadmium Yellow* and *Transparent Kelly Green* next to that. When applying these I also overlapped onto the yellow so the colour shift was gradual, not stark. I didn't want a definitive line where one colour ends and another begins. The overall look was a little bit of the *Testors Model Master Silver Chrome* bleeding through just enough to make the transparent paint look a little metallic. Even though I overlapped the transparent colours so they tied in with each other, I needed to blend them better. I decided to use *Testors MM Graphite Metallic*, which is also transparent, airbrushing on a few thin coats and thus blending all the colours together and toning down the overall silver chrome underneath – achieving the look of stars shimmering from the suit and helmet, the 'star stuff' effect I was looking for. Happy with the results, I airbrushed on several thin coats of *Future* to seal in and protect the paint. When dry, the acrylic finish dried hard, protecting the paint for many years to come. (10-11)

Now it was on to painting the lower part of the base with the 'ALIEN' relief on it and the four cannisters oozing black liquid. Where arms usually would be, just inside the shoulders, the base tangles itself up through the body and slightly shows as weaved bumps on both sides. I really wanted to bring out the detail for the base as much as the body and helmet, achieved by airbrushing *ComArt Transparent Ultramarine* over those areas. After several passes I noticed wherever there were deep crevasses and detail it was nice and dark, which was naturally bringing out a lot more detail and also adding itself as sort of a wash. Once the *Ultramarine* had dried, I applied very light coats of *Transparent Kelly Green* over certain low areas so that, when seen from different views

and depending on the lighting, it would show up as colour variation. Lastly, I used darker transparent blue and purple and airbrushed those colours in high areas to give yet more variation. The intended purpose was to give more colour depth and a 'glow' to the base so that it was unique to itself but didn't distract from or overpower the *Engineer* bust. It was important to show as much detail as possible and to make it look not of this world. (12–13)

The cannisters were next. This part of the build was basic, but a little tedious. So I could easily hold the cannisters while painting, as mentioned above, I drilled small holes into the bottom of each and inserted cut wire hanger rod. I drilled the holes just big enough so the rods were firmly inserted without use of glue – this way, when I was done, I could just slide them out. I airbrushed them with semi-gloss black and let dry overnight, the next day airbrushing *Testors MM Gold* on and again drying overnight. Remember I said these four cannisters were tedious? It had been easy up to this point, but one detail remained… the black ooze, which had to be painted by hand. I used *Testors MM Flat Black* and the thinnest brush I own, my *Loew-Cornell 10/0 7350 Liner*, carefully applying paint around the three dimensional shape

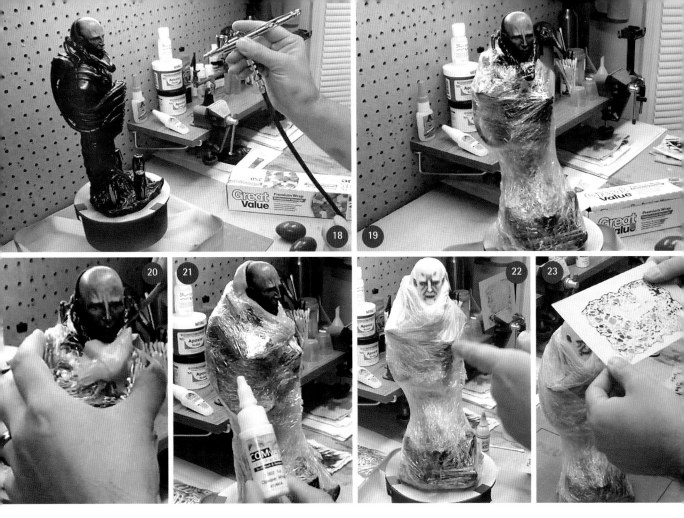

of the ooze. This was long, tedious work – a strain on the eyes and a test of my nerves. After making a complete outline of the ooze on the cannisters, painting got a little easier. The next step was also done by hand using my 000 brush: blocking in the ooze within the outlined areas. Once done, I let dry overnight, sprayed on several thin coats of *Future*, then attached them to the base. (**15-17**)

More than three quarters of the bust was complete, only leaving the head and helmet. I wanted to airbrush the head and make it look as smooth as possible – though a little problem was in my way: I'd already painted the body and base with detail. To avoid any overspray issues while airbrushing, I decided to use a combination of *Silly Putty* and plastic cling wrap. First, I used regular cling wrap that can be bought at any grocery store and gently wrapped it around the painted areas. I did this several times, making sure I had the whole bust covered just under the head. (**18–19**) Second, I made the *Silly Putty* more malleable by 'exercising' it for a few minutes, then applied it around the head. Once I had the *Putty* where I wanted it, I used wooden sculpting tools to help push and form it in areas of detail. The tools only went so far, though, and I was forced to use dental

tools to get into more defined and detailed areas. When the masking was over, the *Engineer* looked like he was wrapped up in a plastic cocoon from the bottom of his head down. Once done to my satisfaction, it was time to paint. (**20–21**) The base colour for the head would be *ComArt Opaque White*. With several coats applied, it was time for detail work. On the face I airbrushed *ComArt Opaque Red* into detailed areas around the eyes, nose and mouth. Next, using *ComArt Opaque Violet* and an organic design stencil from *Iwata*, I airbrushed random veining on top and on both sides of the head. Once dry, I applied several mist coats of the opaque white I'd used as the base colour over the red and violet. This achieved a layered effect, toning down the colours and making them appear to be under the skin. The red turned to a light pink around the eyes and mouth; the violet is barely seen, giving the effect of veins and slightly turning the opaque white purple. This effect gives both human and alien qualities to the *Engineer*'s head. As before, I sprayed on several mists of *Future* and let dry. The end result is a porcelain smooth human/alien hybrid complexion. I finished the head by painting the eyes with *MM Flat Black* and sealed them with a couple coats of

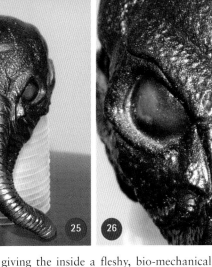

MM Lacquer Finish. **(22–24)** The last detail remained and ties the whole bust together – the helmet.

Over several days I went about painting the helmet the exact same way I'd painted the suit; airbrushing a base of black; silver chrome over that and transparent blue, green and yellow over that, tying the colours together with *MM Graphite Metallic.* And, much like the eyes of the *Engineer*, the helmet's lenses are also black. I sealed it all in with *Future* and let dry. **(25)** I wanted to add the reflection of a galaxy in both lenses, so I airbrushed *Future* heavily onto them so that it would get slightly 'milky' just a little off centre. **(26)** ...Time to flip the helmet over and detail the inside.

As far as detail is concerned, this bust has it in spades. I was very impressed that the inside of the helmet is also well detailed. That said, I wanted to have a little fun and really 'flesh it out'...My idea was to make it look completely different from the rest of the *Engineer*'s suit by giving the inside a fleshy, bio-mechanical look. I painted it all with traditional brushes, laying down a base colour of *Ceramcoat Adobe Red* then dry brushing *Ceramcoat Fleshtone* over that. All the pads were painted with a base colour of *MM Flat Black*, then finished with a couple coats of *MM Graphite Metallic* to tie in with the exterior of the suit. To seal it all in I didn't use *Future*, but went with *MM Semigloss Lacquer* as it gave it a more convincing wet flesh look – again going with a not-of-this-world look, yet something that can still slightly be identified with. **(27)**

That's it – I'm done constructing and painting the *Engineer* kit bust. It's kind of funny when you think about it – constructing an *Engineer*. As the story goes it's the other way around... they constructed us. I hope you enjoyed reading this article and discovered that you can use many different painting techniques and types of paint on a single model. Putting this kit together was easy, but giving myself the painting challenge proved to be... challenging, and that's good. Without challenges we don't grow in the hobby. Thinking outside the box is also good. Just because instructions or box art guide you in a certain direction doesn't mean you have to do things that particular way. Trying different things and going against the grain can be very fulfilling. **(28)**

Jason C. Gares is the Owner and Host of Video Workbench, *and can be contacted at:* jason@videoworkbench.com

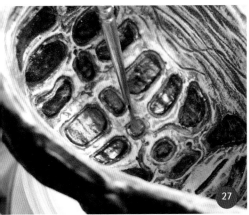

THAT CAR!

1989 Batmobile reissued ...and revisited by Andy Pearson

LONG AGO, WELL ABOUT 1990, I BUILT THIS MODEL ON ITS FIRST TIME ROUND AND DIDN'T DO A VERY GOOD JOB OF IT. I think the main problem was I didn't have access to an airbrush and, being too stupid to use paint from a rattle-can, brush painted the thing. Now I'm aware that some people can produce fantastic results wielding a brush but I'm not one of them.

The original kit came with a variety of chromed parts and I don't know whether this re-issue will have the same feature but the review kit was moulded in an off-white polystyrene and I, for one, would not consider the absence of chromed bits and pieces any great loss as they actually detract from the authenticity of the finished model.

The review kit from *Round 2* arrived (as these things often do) in a plain plastic bag with no instructions and, rather worryingly, no tyres. Fortunately I'm not a chap to throw old models away, instead consigning them to the vault which, in my case, is a small tool shed in the garden.

A search through the mountains of ancient stuff in there resulted in the discovery of what remained of the original kit and entailed the re-housing of

several spiders but provided me with the original tyres and the chromed wheels which would be of use later.

Assuming that the new kit I now had was an early pull from the moulds, I gave it a fairly close examination to see what might be needed in terms of clean-up. There were some areas on the driver's side front wing that needed filling and smoothing and some sections of the kit had thin coatings of green and light brown discolouration that I assumed to be traces of some sort of mould release agents. These were easily removed using the methylated spirit which I used to clean all the parts in anticipation of priming.

For the main body of the *Batmobile* I used *Vallejo* grey surface primer applied via my airbrush. For some of the separate panels, specifically the machine gun and grappling iron housings, I primed with *Halfords* grey primer as I thought that a slightly different finish to these might make for an interesting effect.

Despite having built the original model some 25 years ago and having no instructions the assembly promised to be reasonably straightforward and this was helped by two factors. One was the fit of

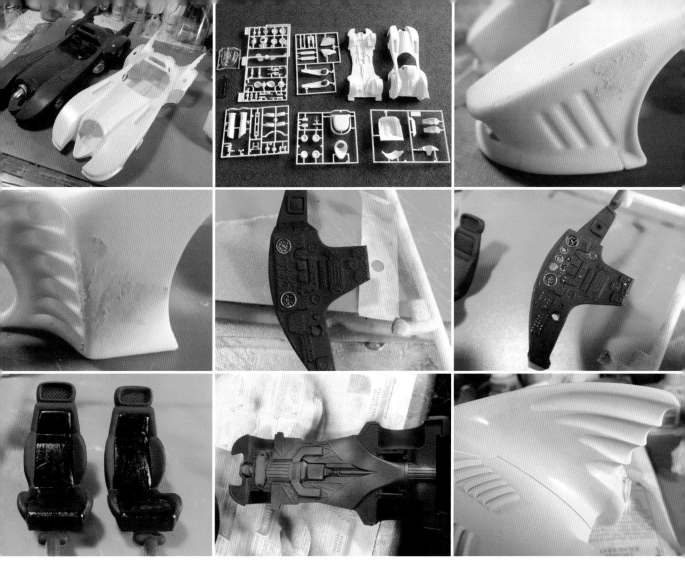

Top row: The new
kit body compared
with the old model.
The parts supplied
with the new kit.
Filler to front wing.

Centre row: More
filler to body.
Highlighting dials
with the help of
masks.
Detailing to
dashboard.

Row above: Matt
and semi-gloss
paint to seats.
Contrasting paint
textures to intakes.
Cleaned-up rear
wing.

the parts, which was excellent, and the other by having on my bookshelves a copy of **Batmobile: The Complete History** by Mark Cotta Vas. This is a wonderful book and covers the various versions of the titular vehicle in comics, TV and on film.

I was, perhaps obviously, keen to improve on the finish of my earlier effort which, in truth, looked as though it was a scale version of a car painted using a 4-inch brush. There was also the question of just how glossy the finish would be, the fact that it was black being a given. Amongst the images in the aforementioned book was a wonderful gatefold spread of photographs that resulted from documentary film makers Roko Belic and Tara Tremaine bringing together all five movie versions of the *Batmobile* and the TV version on the *Warner's* studio lot.

It was evident from those that the car we are looking at here was the least glossy of all, apart from the *Tumbler*. With those references to hand I began to experiment with paint finishes. My

model paint of choice has been, for many years, *Tamiya* acrylic, so using *X-18 Semi-Gloss Black* as my starting point I began to test various mixtures, adding gloss black, matt and thinners in various proportions. In the end I used the semi-gloss version thinned 50/50 which seemed to work quite well, although I did have a trick up my sleeve which I wanted to try once the paint was completely dry.

Whilst the bodywork was drying I airbrushed the underside of the car in matt black with a misting of gun metal (my own mix) to pick out the detail. Flat black was also used for the entire cockpit interior including the dashboard, although I used un-thinned semi-gloss black for sections of the seats which would be leather. Here I brush-painted those areas, ignoring all the rules designed to produce an even finish as I wanted to get some texture.

The dashboard features in its own spread in the **Batmobile** book and so I was provided with the

very best references for detailing this. Now it may be that the release kit will be provided with decals for instrumentation although I don't think that the original did as I probably would have used those way back when.

In this case I punched holes of several sizes in *Tamiya* masking tape and used these as masks for the dials which I then dry-brushed in off-white to bring out the moulded detail. Various other controls were then picked out in reds and yellows using a sharpened cocktail stick and thinned acrylics. With the dials dry, I gave each a slight gloss using *Games Workshop* clear varnish and the effect was quite pleasing although not, I fear, up to the standards that our military modelling friends achieve.

I now had several key components set aside to dry and therefore had the leisure to study some sections of the kit that had puzzled from the start. Provided with the *Round 2* kit were parts for what was almost certainly a gas-turbine type of engine,

an additional component that seemed to fit this and one or two other odds and ends. On the inside of the forward floor-pan (under the bonnet or hood on the completed model) were four plastic columns. As these didn't serve as connectors for the main body of the car to sit on it seemed as though they might be mounting points for the engine but I couldn't work out how they would work in this context.

In the end I set the engine components aside as interesting curiosities and await the kit's commercial release with interest. There were also two grille inserts obviously destined to sit in front of the windscreen as air intakes for the cockpit, as on most modern vehicles. As these were already moulded into the bonnet (or hood) their purpose remains a mystery as do several curved panels that had what I assume to be instrumentation moulded into their surfaces.

The other redundant parts, as far as this build was concerned, were two wing-mounted

Top row: Side panel and intake pieces. Main engine intake and *Batmissile*. A selection of panels, intakes and filler caps.

Central row: Initial paint job to body. *Tamiya Smoke* to windshield. Chromed wheels with semi-gloss black acrylic.

Row above: Wheels, tyres and high-lighted *Bat-logo*. Cockpit components. Seats and some control details in place.

Top row: Cockpit.
Jet exhaust.
Masking to machine
gun housing panels.

Central row: Reduced
contrast paint
texture on panels.
Completed chassis
and wheels.
Aluminium foil
reflectors to
headlights.

Row above: Cockpit
bulkhead panel.
Alternative cockpit
view.
Paint texture
contrasts viewed
from the front.

machine guns and a grappling hook which seemed a little too big for the hinged panels I assume it was intended to occupy. I imagine that this might serve the modeller who wished to duplicate the movie scene when the *Batmobile* makes a sharp turn by firing a hawser round a piece of street furniture.

The machine guns presented the opportunity for some further paint experiments. Two of the chromed parts in the original 1989 kit that actually appeared to be chrome on the real thing were the inserts just in front of the main intakes on the forward body. Again, I didn't want these to be too shiny and so thought that I might use one of the enamels from the *Humbrol Metalcote* range, specifically *27003 Polished Steel*. Forgive me if you already know this but these are paints that dry to a dull finish but then can be polished up using cloth, paper tissue or even cotton buds to give a very realistic metallic finish without that grain that one sometimes gets with similar acrylics. Having found this experiment a success I airbrushed the

same paint onto the inserts and polished away after twenty minutes or so of drying time.

The *Batmobile's* headlights were supplied as moulded units with clear inserts and, as I was still killing time until the paint on the bodywork was thoroughly dry, it seemed reasonable to spend some time productively here. Instead of painting the inserts' reflectors silver it occurred to me that some reflective foil might give them an extra gleam so I cut two trapezoid shapes and glued these within using thin PVA before inserting the lenses.

The final step before main assembly was painting the wheels and fitting the tyres. As I was trying to achieve the same colour values as the original car I thought it might be interesting to try something using the chromed wheels from the original model. The thought process here was to *a)* see what the semi-gloss black would look like on top of the chrome and *b)* discover whether the moulded bat logo on each hub could be emphasised by removing the paint on that area to

let the chrome show through. I think I can claim some success on both fronts.

With the paint on the bodywork now having had almost a full week to dry, I inserted the cockpit assembly and the body panels that I had primed with the *Halfords* grey and airbrushed gloss black, despite my earlier plan. The cockpit fitted beautifully but the contrasting panels presented, well, too much of a contrast. I therefore masked round these in-situ and airbrushed them with my semi-gloss black mixture. There was still a very slight difference in their refractive qualities due to the differing primer and the gloss undercoat but this was subtle and that's what I'd been after.

With the bodywork paintjob now completely dry it was time to try the trick that I mentioned

earlier. Studio lighting, like moonlight, can be cruelly deceptive, Amanda, as the images in the **Batmobile** book showed only too well, with the reflective quality of the bodywork varying almost shot for shot. There are many and varied possible reasons for that. When I'm not doing this (i.e. boring you with my ramblings about models) I frequently write scripts for TV commercials. Sometimes, usually when an underpaid and overaged 'gopher' is needed, I get to go on the shoots. Lighting cameramen (and women) don't, as a rule, like reflective surfaces as they tend to reflect that which is best left un-reflected. Sometimes the problem is overcome with careful angles, sometimes with clever concealment techniques, occasionally with dulling sprays and, nowadays, by painting out unwanted reflections in post-production. You can, perhaps, picture the

Top left: Rear view with spare transparent parts in foreground.

Finished model with roof removed.

potential problem: a dramatic shot of a gleaming Batmobile with the film crew, including two grips playing cards, reflected on the beautiful bodywork.

Notwithstanding those considerations one would assume a little stealth capability would benefit a crime fighting vehicle (Get to the point! Ed.)

In order to achieve the correct balance with this model I'd decided to see what a little judicious polishing might do. This was simply a matter of gently rubbing away at selected curves and contours with a paper kitchen towel to bring out some highlights. The technique is simplicity itself BUT there are a couple of basic rules to be observed. Overdo it and you're back to the primer (I actually did this for real whilst working on a bodywork repair on my trusty Cruiser). Change the area of paper you are polishing with regularly as the towel itself becomes polished to some extent

and loses its efficacy. The third rule (suggestion might be a better word) applies if you have a paper towel that has some dry overspray from your original airbrush work on it. The areas with this dry paint seem to act as a very gentle abrasive and aid the polishing – but do see rule one!

The final stages of construction were to fit the rear lights (lots of spares provided with my kit), the rear jet exhaust outlet, the distinctive front with what the reference book refers to as the Bat-missile and the canopy with the windshield airbrushed in *Tamiya X-19 Smoke*.

I'm looking forward to seeing this kit again when it's released (no hints as to when on the *Round 2* website at the time of writing) if only to discover what all the extra bits and pieces are for.

Review test shot kindly supplied by
Round 2 Models.
www.round2models.com

In the concluding part of his '60s' movie Time Machine *build, Jason assembles the remaining pieces and explains how to super-detail and paint Masterpiece Models' replica kit to perfection...*

'Working' *Time Machine* kit replicas feature blinking console lights and a spinning disc controlled by a board inside the console. Several parts need to be soldered to this, the very specific instructions supplied helping put it all together. Time, patience and an above-basic understanding of electronics is helpful. If wanting to build a working example of this kit for yourself make sure, wherever you decide to solder the board together, that it and the room are free of animal hair, dust and static. Once complete check it fits inside the console and all wires get to their respective areas without problems – more wire is better than not enough. (1–2.) Lastly, if building a working version I fit a small motor, which drives the disc, into a case, place case and motor inside the generator housing, screw two small lightbulbs on either side of an arm and epoxy that to the case top, making sure the lightbulbs stick out as they slightly sit inside the transparent cones on each side.

At this stage in my project the generator was prepped and put aside so that I could continue with the rest of the build...(3.) ...The twenty-part seat is a kit all its own and was next up for assembly. You can go strictly by the instructions here or find your own way. When sub-assemblies are put together, however, bear in mind how you plan on

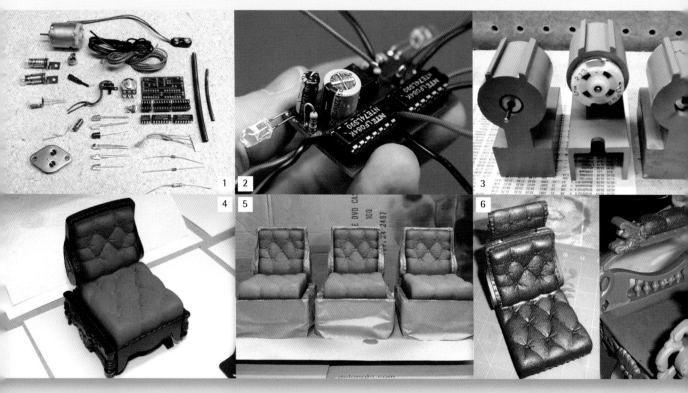

Tripping Through Time

Jason C. Gares moves through the years to perfect construction of Masterpiece Models' Time Machine kit.

Part two of two.

painting parts afterwards. If not careful, after gluing certain parts together, you could find an area you won't be able to paint. I began by airbrushing all parts needing a wood grain look with thinned down *Ceramcoat Burnt Umber* acrylic. I then applied coats of *Future* to seal the paint and let dry for a few days. (4.) Next, I applied painters tape over the areas previously painted *Umber*, exposing back, seat, arm and head cushions. (5.) I airbrushed those areas with *MM British Crimson* then, in the crevasses, airbrushed *MM Flat Black* and let dry, misting the *Crimson* lightly over the black to give depth to the cushion areas. This is commonly known as pre-shading, used to highlight panel lines on aircraft, military vehicles and spaceships. (6.) I felt the cushion buttons were not defined enough and needed replacing, accomplishing this by drilling

Sometimes clients want more of a fabric look to the cushions, achieved using *Micro Metal Foil Adhesive*, maroon flocking by *Detail Master* and *MM British Crimson* enamel. (8.) I apply the flocking before taking off the painters tape from airbrushing the *Crimson* directly onto the part so I can achieve straight lines where defined. Remember, whatever colour flocking you use, the colour underneath needs to be close to it. First, using a brush, I apply a thin layer of *Micro Metal Foil Adhesive* on all cushion areas. A little at a time, in small sections, I sprinkle the flocking on. When a cushion is completely covered I lightly press the flocking into the glue and let sit overnight. When dry, I lightly brush off any flocking that did not adhere to the glue. (9.) As before, I drill holes for the buttons but before

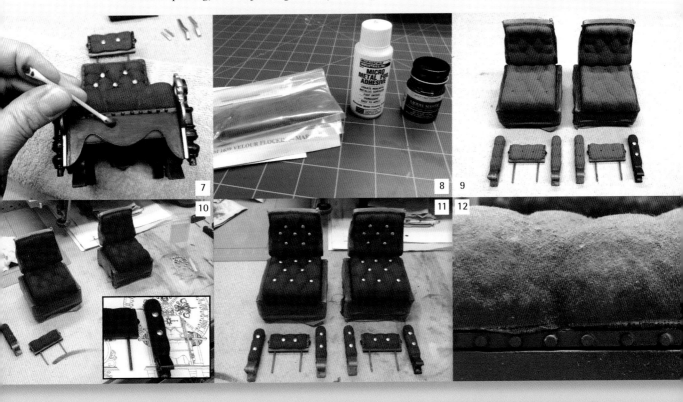

holes in the areas where buttons should be and epoxying in 1¼" cut-down carpet trim nails. Going back to the parts painted *Burnt Umber* and wanting those areas to look closer to stained wood, using a brush I generously applied *ComArt Transparent Black* over them and let sit for a couple of days. I then took cotton swabs dipped in *Createx Colors Airbrush Reducer* and wiped back and forth, leaving streaks and areas that made the paint look more like stained wood. Also, the *Transparent Black* got into crevasses and around detailed areas... when wiped away with the swab, more detail was noticed. (7.)

adding the carpet trim nails I airbrush *Crimson* over the flocking with very low air pressure so as not to blow off any loose flocking. (10 & inset.) I cut the carpet nails down with my motor tool and glue them into the holes. (11.) Once the cushions are dry, using my hobby blade I carefully cut away the painters tape. When cutting, sometimes the blade finds a spot and travels, cutting into areas I don't want it to. (12.) This is easily remedied by adding more flocking or painting the affected section. I finish by painting the gold carpet nails *Crimson* to match the rest of the cushions, gluing the headrest on top of the back cushion, attaching with epoxy the armrests to both sides and painting the nails with *MM Gold* enamel, completing the seat. (13.)

Back at the base, I prepped the foot pad for painting and flocking application. As with the seats, I began with grey primer and followed up by masking off the rest of the base, only exposing the foot pad. Once finished, I airbrushed on *MM Crimson* and let dry. For the painted version I generously apply *ComArt Transparent Black* over the pad, let dry and wipe off using a cotton swab dipped in *Createx Colors Airbrush Reducer*. (14a–14b.) If working on a flocked version, I skip the last step and apply *Micro Metal Foil Adhesive* instead of *Black*. Before the adhesive dries, I apply the same flocking I applied to the seat cushions, press into the glue and let dry overnight. The next day

and/or plastic baggies. Both can be sealed, preventing loss, damage and dust on parts. Also, keeping parts ready for assembly and paint away from other parts is essential. I've learned if you stay organised while building and painting you'll have more fun and an easier time with assembly. Work smarter, not harder. (16.)The build gets a little tricky at this point, so pinning was essential to keep it all together and sturdy. The generator housing was epoxied down and screwed to the base from the top and the generator cones were epoxied into the housing. (17.) The seat was also epoxied and screwed down to the base, but from the bottom. Having seat and generator housing centered is key to it all fitting on the base correctly. There's a template that can be cut out and placed on top of the base, with holes drawn on it so you

I brush off any loose flocking and apply more if needed. I then airbrush *Crimson* over the flocking, pull off the masking and finish the pad by painting the bolts/rivets gold. Now the foot pad looks like it has actual fabric sewn into it and matches the seat. (15.) Side note: it's important to keep all parts well organised and protected while building this elaborate replica. After putting together sub-assemblies, proper storage is a factor that shouldn't be overlooked. There are many parts to this kit that are painted the same colour and can be grouped together in the stages you want to build them. I suggest plastic storage containers

know where to place both seat and generator housing. Holes have to be drilled completely through the base, which can be done at the beginning of the build, prior to painting, to avoid chipping. If you decide to drill holes after painting, place painters tape where you need to on the base before drilling to avoid chipping paint and splintering the base. Test fit both vertical rails, as the generator cones need to seed into them. If the ends of the cones are too wide, the rear circular section of the rails will have to be bored out more to make them fit, accomplished using grinding bits attached to a motor tool. Go slow. Make sure the

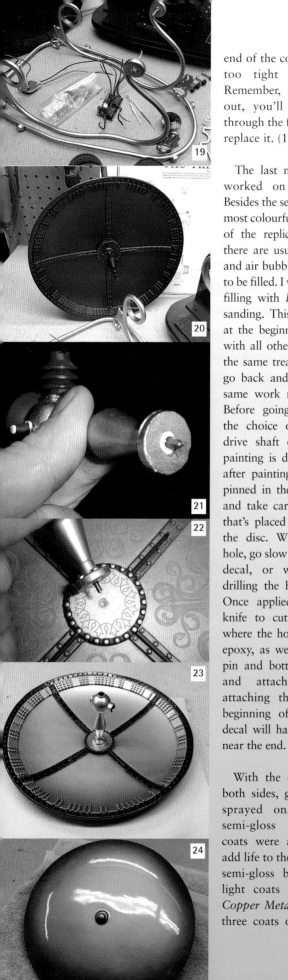

end of the cone fits snug, not too tight or too loose. Remember, if a bulb burns out, you'll need to go in through the front of a cone to replace it. (18–20.)

The last major part to be worked on was the disc. Besides the seat, it's the largest, most colourful and ornate part of the replica. As it's resin, there are usually pour spouts and air bubble holes that need to be filled. I work these out by filling with *Bondo* then wet-sanding. This is usually done at the beginning of the build with all other parts that need the same treatment, as to not go back and forth doing the same work more than once. Before going further, there's the choice of attaching the drive shaft or waiting until painting is done. If attaching after painting, make sure it's pinned in the absolute centre and take care with the decal that's placed in the centre of the disc. When drilling the hole, go slow as to not tear the decal, or wait until after drilling the hole to apply it. Once applied, use a hobby knife to cut out the centre where the hole is. Fill it with epoxy, as well as around the pin and bottom of the shaft and attach. (21–22.) If attaching the shaft at the beginning of the build, the decal will have to be applied near the end.

With the disc smooth on both sides, grey primer was sprayed on, followed by semi-gloss black. Colour coats were applied next to add life to the piece. Over the semi-gloss black I sprayed light coats of *Rust-Oleum Copper Metallic*, sealed with three coats of *Future*. Once

dry and using painters tape, I masked off the shaft and rest of the disc leaving only the outer rim and cross beams exposed, as they would be sprayed with *DupliColor Cordova Brown Metallic*. Only two coats were needed, also sprayed with *Future* to seal in the colour. More *Future* was applied to smooth it out and further protect the paint. (23–24.) Detail painting was next on the list. *Thinned Ceramcoat Hunter Green* was gently brushed over the round, raised centre area in the middle of the disc (where the drive shaft is located), followed by *MM Gold* on top of that, sealed with *Future*. After a few days, making sure the *Future* had hardened, on top of the four crossbeams I formed triangles using *Tamiya* pinstriping tape and painters tape. I sprayed several mists of *MM Gold* and lifted off the tape shortly thereafter, painted *Hunter Green* on the raised triangles that connect to the centre and did any touch-up work necessary. (25-27.)

With final paint finished, it was time to apply the decals. I cut these as close to the graphic as possible (28.) (If I'd attached the drive shaft at the initial building stage, then I'd fit the decal that goes there around it, accomplished by using a hole puncher, cutting a hole in the centre.) (29.) Still on the backing I cut the decal in half, dipped one side

33 |

at a time in water, applied *Micro Sol* to the area the decal was to go on, slid it onto the centre of the disc and repeated with the other side. *Micro Sol* applied to both decals allows me to move them closer to each other so they look like one decal. I applied *Micro Set* and let dry, repeating this process with the eight larger decals that are placed in the four pie sections. With all decals applied, I airbrushed *Future* over them to get rid of the edges, giving the illusion they were painted on and protecting them. (30.) Final assembly was accomplished in no particular order. I'd already attached the generator cones to the housing, housing and seat to the base and shaft to the disc. The door to the back of the generator housing needed gluing on and the rubber wheel to the motor's shaft (for the working version) so the disc

replica, before attaching the rails, decals need to be applied to both ends where the 'leaf like' designs are located – just above the balls in the bottom curled areas. Also, running in the centre of both rails are *Hunter Green* stripes. This adds time to the build, but makes it more accurate. Working version rails have wires coming out so they can be attached to the board inside the console; non-working don't. Before attaching the console to both rails I make sure the working version has appropriate coloured LEDs installed to the electronics board. The static version has resin pieces simulating the bulbs. Cages are constructed for the three lights with the wire provided. Decals for specific times in the movie are represented by month/day/year with green, yellow and red decals. In working versions these light up. (32.)

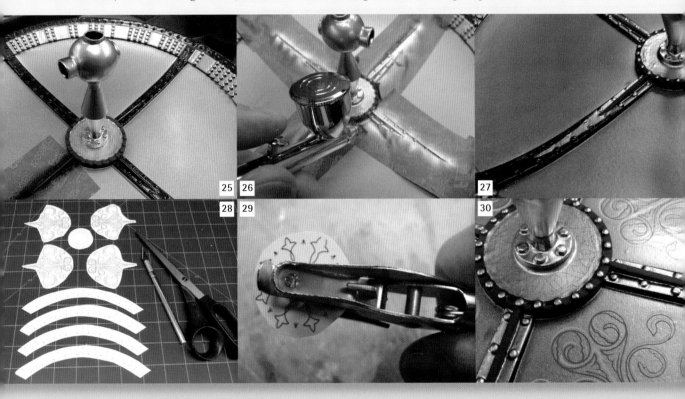

could lean on something, as to not bend the connection between drive shaft and generator housing and allow the disc to spin. For non-working versions everything is permanently epoxied in place. The two red, green and yellow copper coils needed to be attached to their like-coloured cones on either side, between the drive shaft and generator housing. A red beacon light and cage were epoxied to the very top of the drive shaft. For working versions, wires need to be threaded through and an LED light placed in the same area. (31.)The two vertical rails attach to the end of the generator cones. For a more ornate

The key/lever is in three parts: body, crystal and thin rod connecting these together. I had painted the body marble blue, but discovered later it's marble green. Above and below the body I painted *MM Gold*. I drilled a small hole into the centre of the body and epoxied the thin rod inside it, then the crystal over that. On the static version the key/lever doesn't move; on the working version it's connected to a potentiometer that determines output of current to the board inside the console, which is connected to the motor in the generator housing through the wires in the rails. Moving the key/lever up from the down position makes the

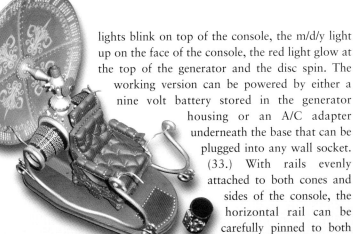

lights blink on top of the console, the m/d/y light up on the face of the console, the red light glow at the top of the generator and the disc spin. The working version can be powered by either a nine volt battery stored in the generator housing or an A/C adapter underneath the base that can be plugged into any wall socket. (33.) With rails evenly attached to both cones and sides of the console, the horizontal rail can be carefully pinned to both vertical rails and generator cone caps. Before attaching the rail, as with the vertical rails, it's suggested to paint a *Hunter Green* stripe on the very centre of the rail, all the way

centred, the horizontal rail shouldn't touch the disc on either side or from behind. (36.)

That's it: *complete*. To make this a little more unique, you could make a checkered base to represent the lab floor from the movie, or a reproduction of the box the miniature prototype was carried in... It all depends what you are looking for to make it as close to the movie prop as possible. You can find the kit at: MasterpieceModels.com for $179.99 USD (electronics upgrade kit $325.00 USD).

Thank you for reading. If you have questions on how to build this kit or would like one built, please contact me at: jason@videoworkbench.com.

around. There are also five stripes – 1 thick, 4 thin – in front and behind the four ornate knobs where the connections are made to be pinned to the model. The outside of these are also painted *Hunter Green*, though using green pinstriping tape may be a faster, more accurate way to apply the pinstriping on the three rails. (34a–34b.)

The final part to attach was the ornate bar that connects underneath the console and to both vertical rails. Pin and epoxy it in place making sure it's centred at the correct angle, do touch-up painting if necessary. (35.) If the rails are properly

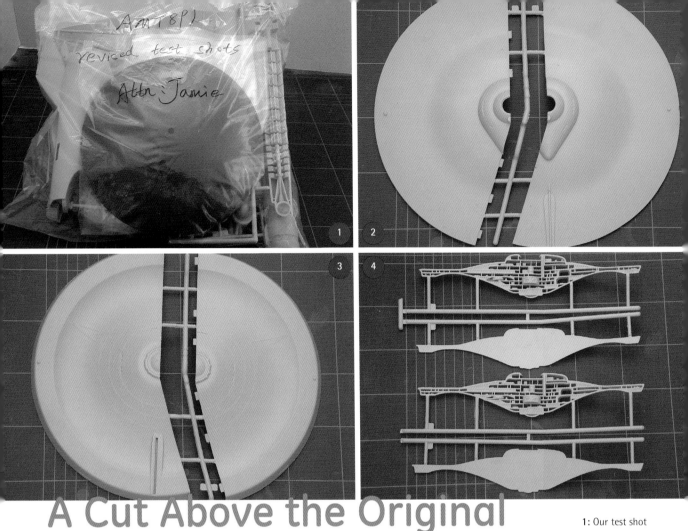

A Cut Above the Original

Gary R. Welsh tells the inside story of Round 2's Trek re-release

I MUST ADMIT TO BEING SOMEWHAT TAKEN ABACK WHEN I LEARNED THAT THE *U.S.S. ENTERPRISE CUTAWAY NCC-1701 1/537 SCALE KIT WAS TO BE REISSUED*. It really is a '*Marmite*' model, with some modellers loving it and many others regarding it with derision. Thinking about it, though, the kit was originally released for **Star Trek**'s 30th. anniversary, and, as we approach **Trek**'s 50th., I suppose it only seems logical that it should again see light of day.

First off let's place this kit into an historical context. At the time of its release *Polar Lights'* amazing 1/350th *Enterprise* was not available and neither was the eye-wateringly expensive *DeBoars* kit. The only game in town then was the ageing 18" *AMT Enterprise* first released in the late 1960s; the tiny 1/2500th version, and small-scale *FASA* and *Comet* white metal kits. As a result, when *AMT/Ertl* announced that they would be releasing a 22" new-tool *Enterprise* many modellers were understandably excited.

When the kit arrived (back in the day), I built a test shot of it for a shop window and it became apparent that, although the 'cutaway' concept seemed like a good idea, it did not in reality work on any level as the pull-away parts located poorly and the *warp pylons* needed to be reinforced with brass rod to stop them sagging. In short, the model was a complete disaster!

...Nevertheless it was still, at the time, as accurate a 22" *Enterprise* as you could build out of the box and I ended up building over twenty of these kits as various commissions ...but as complete ships without the gimmicky cutaway parts.

Nearly twenty years down the line, if you are looking for a super-accurate TV *Enterprise* look no further than *Polar Lights'* awesome 1/350th kit. If considering an economical alternative to that release, however, how does this model shape up today, being something of a curiosity?

1: Our test shot arrived in a sealed bag, complete with notes.

2 & 3: Close-ups of the *primary hull* parts. The tabs seem to have been amended compared to how I remember this kit being (and I've built enough of them in the past!)

4: Reissued parts (top of frame), with original parts bottom of frame (I have a few of these to hand in the spares box). The reissued parts seem to be sharper, so the moulds may well have been amended.

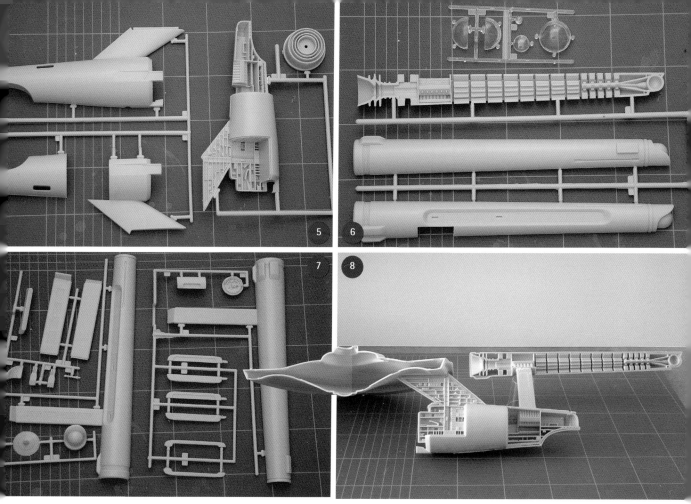

5: *Secondary hull parts – again sharp detail with clean mouldings.*

6: *Cutaway nacelle parts (along with clear parts).*

7: *Remaining parts. Pylons have been strengthened and location points amended... Hurrah!*

8: *Completed whole half section of model. Point where nacelle meets pylon has been strengthened with brass rod epoxied in place. No other modifications were required. Fit was above what I expected – a pleasant surprise – only took an hour to get to this point.*

The test shot arrived bagged and without decals (which I'm sure will be top notch when they become available). Upon opening the bag and examining the contents it immediately became apparent that Jamie Hood and his team had spent a lot of time reengineering and cleaning up the moulds. In fact this was the cleanest copy of this kit that I have ever seen ...remarkable!

The release is, in essence, the same as the original, although the *warp pylons* have been strengthened with the addition of cross members on the underside of the *pylon* halves. The *pylon* attachment points have also been altered, but unfortunately the original stand (complete with awesome *Starfleet* symbol that looked great painted in antique bronze) has been replaced with a standard *Polar Lights* round version.

Considering the care and attention that *Polar Lights* have lavished on this release, I decided that it was only fair that I build mine as the cutaway display model it is intended to be. Construction began with the main part, or complete half, of the ship. Assembly was rapid and the fit very positive. I didn't, however, fit the *deflector* parts or the

saucer cutaway detailing and *bridge* as these sections would be painted and added later, during final construction.

The only addition I made was brass rod, secured in place with *Devcon 5-ton Epoxy* as the location tab was a little shallow, and used to pin the engine half along with its detail insert.

The removable section of the *secondary hull* was then constructed, the fit of which was really good. However, when attached to the main part of the model the section began to sag dramatically, so I had to come up with a way of producing an interesting display ...and this is where the new stand came up trumps.

Addressing the removable parts it was obvious that the engine and *saucer section* parts were going to be something of a headache and unlikely to inspire any practical solution. Luckily I had a cunning plan for these (see *Romulan BOP* review last issue for details).

At this stage brass rod and aluminium tubing were employed. I epoxied the tubing onto the back

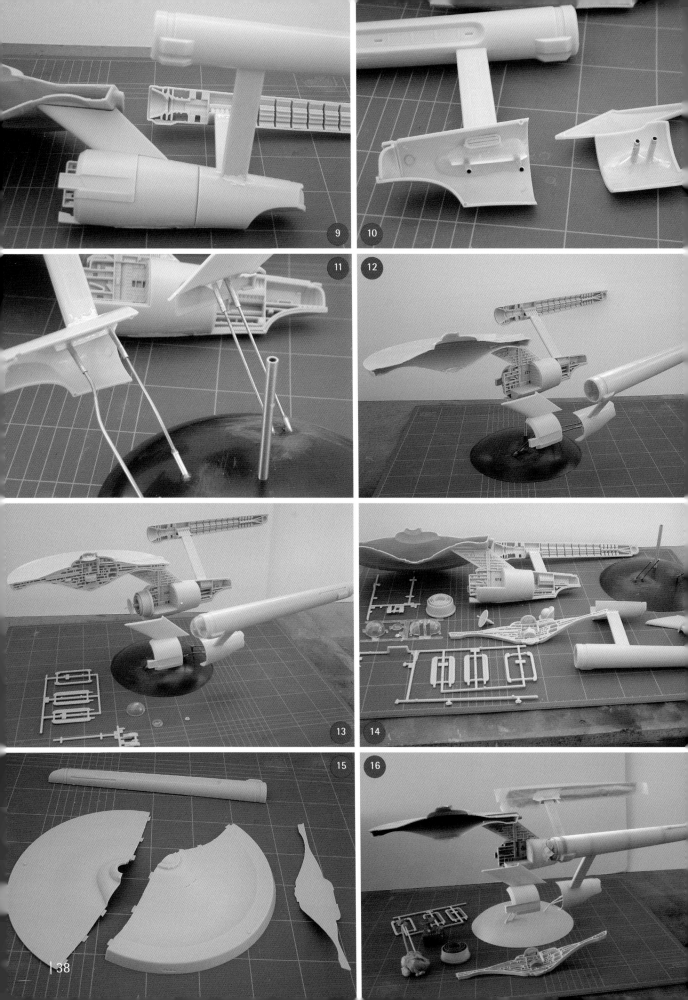

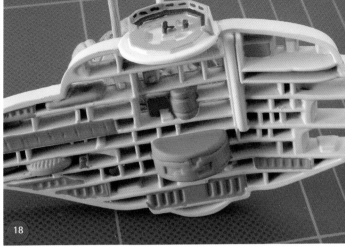
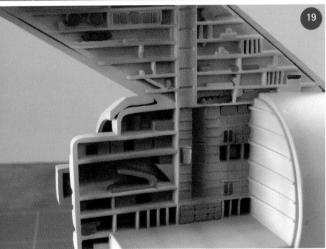
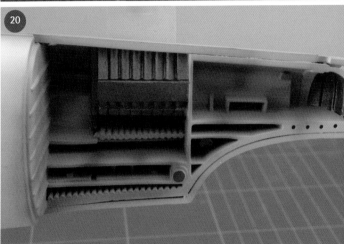

9: Unfortunately the fit of the removable parts is still on the poor side and they don't locate or lock in place positively when placed on the stand. You can't have everything, however... time for an alternative set up. 10: The first stage of the amendment to the display is to add these aluminium tubes embedded into epoxy. 11: Brass rod (which fitted the aluminium tubing snugly) was then epoxied into the new display stand. The removal of the original (stunning) *Starfleet* emblem stand actually makes this easier than it would be otherwise. 12: The main parts test-fitted on the stand. Looking good so far. 13: Final test-fit of all the parts before they are all stripped off and everything is primed in *Alclad Matt Black Micro Filler and Primer*. 14: All parts stripped ready for paint. 15: Rack my brains as I did, I couldn't find a use for these parts so they are spare. 16: With the basic painting done on the interior parts the model is readied for external detail and weathering. 17: The *saucer* interior part with basic painting complete, along with the *nacelle fin*, *deflector* and *dish*. 18: Close-up of the *saucer* detail parts. Note the extra paint detail added to the *bridge*. I feel a *ParaGrafix* detail set on the way... 19: Neck and front, *secondary hull* detail with basic painting added. 20: *Engineering* and *hanger deck*, which is begging for a *shuttle* to put in it!

of each of the removable parts and then carefully cut the brass, inserted it into the tubing and positioned the parts on the stand. I marked where I needed to drill location holes then epoxied them into the stand. Once fully cured the brass was bent and cut to achieve its final position.

This done it was time for some filling and sanding which, compared to the work required on the original-release cutaway kits I have built, was next to nothing. The model was then assembled on its stand for final adjustments before being disassembled and primed in *Alclad Matt Black*

Primer Filler in readiness for paint.

My main colour of choice is *Halfords Casablanca Daewoo White*, which is now no longer available! I used up my last cans on this build, meaning I will now need to get a batch of the paint matched at an automotive supplier. This is going to be pricey, but easier and cheaper in the long run than having cans mixed to order.

Once dry, the finish was sealed in *Liquitex Matte Varnish* and the model shaded in *Vallejo Sky*. Internal details were then picked out in various colours using original *AMT* box artwork as a guide. Some careful airbrushing was also required to bring the *warp nacelle* detail to life using *Liquitex Soft Body Acrylics* as the colours are pure with no grey tones. I then added external details using *Vallejo Dark Sea Grey* and *Light Grey*. The characteristic yellow ring was also applied to the *saucer* and the deflector painted *Copper*.

The *Bussard collectors* were painted as per the 1/1000th *Enterprise and Botany Bay* kit reviewed back in Volume 31. As there were no decals available, I only added some generic red coachlines with hand-painted yellow *Starfleet* insignia.

The edges of the removable sections were painted in *Vallejo Dark Sea Grey* and all parts were then sealed with *Liquitex Matt Varnish*. The edges on the inside section of the *Bussard collector* were picked out in *Liquitex Orange* to suggest a bit of heat and make them stand out. The stand was given a solid coat of *Halfords Matt Black*, final assembly was carried out, the model parts were placed on the stand... and the build was complete.

In conclusion, I enjoyed building this model much more than I thought I would. *Round 2* have done a great job in cleaning up the moulds, and in strengthening and improving the fit. It's just a pity that the cutaway sections still don't fit together and hold in place well on the finished model. This, however, would have meant major amendments to the tooling which would probably have made the reissue uneconomical. That tiny niggle aside, a little imagination and a bit of work – a good way to wile away a few afternoons – will produce an excellent, large desktop display model you can be proud of at a reasonable price.

As stated, I had a great time building this kit. It was a blast – and on that basis alone I thoroughly recommend this release to all. Very well done, *Round 2*.

My very grateful thanks to Jamie Hood for supplying the test shot for this review. You made this old modeller a very happy man!

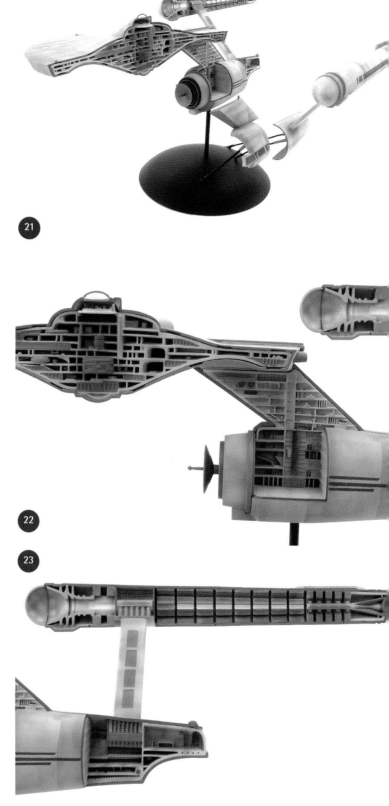

21: The completed model – stunning! **22:** Detail shot of the middle section of the cutaway half. **23:** Close-up shot of the cutaway *nacelle*. Careful airbrushed shading and hand painting here will really pay dividends. **24:** Without any other parts – the cutaway half of the model. **25:** Side on shot of the non-cutaway side of the model.

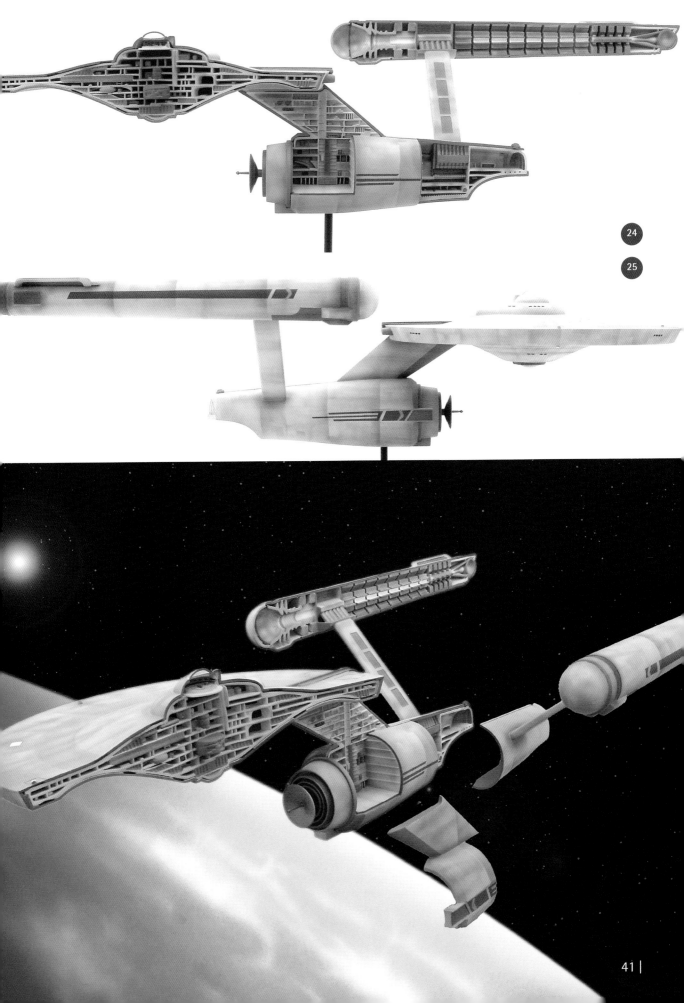

UNDER PRESSURE

GARY R. WELSH EXPLAINS WHY, AFTER CONSIDERING A CHANGE OF AIRBRUSH SET-UP, HE'S MADE A SERIOUS INVESTMENT IN IWATA

HAVING BEEN MODELLING FOR THE LAST 46 YEARS, IT WILL PROBABLY COME AS A SURPRISE TO MOST OF YOU THAT I HAVE ONLY USED AN AIRBRUSH FOR THE LAST 23 – for modelling, that is. Until that point I had only ever airbrushed artwork, having been trained to use this amazing tool at the age of 17 when I was an apprentice.

Since that time I have used virtually every type of airbrush known to man, starting out on *Devillbis* (*Sprite*, *Fischer* and *Sprayguns*), *Humbrol*, *Badger* (100, 150 and 200), *Thayler & Chandler* (under the *Revell* brand), *Aztek* (all types), *Rotring* (*Conopois*), *Harder & Steenback* (*Evolution*), *Iwata* (*Revolution*) and *Paasche* (*F, H, V, VL, Talon*).

Of late I have been using cheap *Iwata* copies from China produced by *Fengda* and available from a variety of outlets under various brand names and these have served me well. Until now, that is...

My father was always trying to buy me a state of the art *Iwata*, even though I knew deep down I really didn't need one. After all, tools do not make the artist... buying a 1st grade violinist a

Stradivarius will not instantly make them an international concert virtuoso, just as buying a driver who has recently passed their test a *Ferrari* could be seen as stupidly irresponsible.

This having been said, when my father sadly passed away last year I decided, as I would (under the worst set of circumstances) be coming into some money, I would very much like to buy something Dad would have really wanted me to have and would remind me of him each time I used it. I therefore decided it was time to completely overhaul my airbrush set-up with something that would last me the remainder of my modelling lifetime.

In-depth research

I began by researching what are deemed to be the absolute best airbrushes on the market: *Richpen* and a Japanese

Top: the *G5* in action on a **Trek** subject. Opposite: airbrusing a *Bussard Ramscoop* on the *Cutaway Enterprise*. See p36.

1: The *Maxx Jet* compressor – a compact box in which is a powerful compressor producing 1.4CFM, capable of running 2 brushes or a mini-spraygun with room to spare, at a relatively modest price.

1A: Opening the box reveals all sorts of goodies. The airbrush and spraygun holders come as standard along with 2 x 3m air hoses, a regulator and a storage tray.

1B: The *Neo TRN-1*. *Iwata*'s budget pistol grip brush fitted with a 0.35mm head and needle set (a standard gravity *Neo Brush* is available for as little as £50).

2: What's in the box: two sizes of paint cup and a wrench for the nozzle – although this should only ever be removed if absolutely necessary.

3: The *Hi-Line HP-BH*.

4: What's inside the box; although lube is included, it's advisable to buy a larger tube as keeping the airbrush clean and well maintained is very worthwhile.

4A: The business end of the *HP-BH*, the MAC valve (the quick release female fitting is extra at a very reasonable £7).

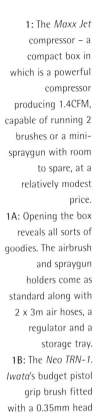

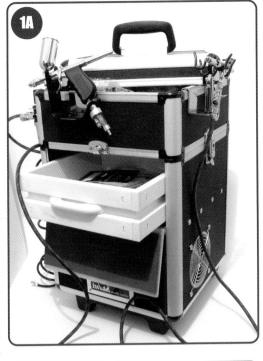

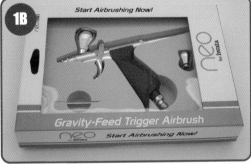

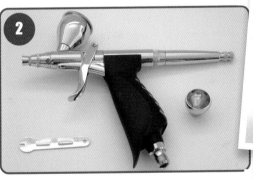

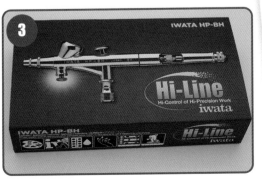

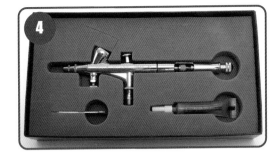

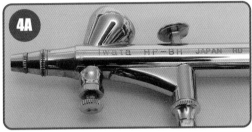

handmade brush company were recommended. However, one manufacturer's products kept coming up again and again in my research – *Iwata*. I had used an *Iwata* airbrush before, but was – to be absolutely honest- not impressed by the performance for the price. Then again, mine was one of the cheapest in the range and I was comparing it to a *Devillbis Fischer F* – so maybe I was being

IWATA KUSTOM CS

ECLIPSE CS

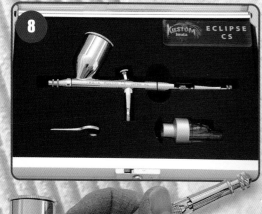

somewhat over critical. Feedback and reviews were hard to ignore, but I was loathe to part with money on such a large investment without trying out the products first.

By a stroke of luck the *Iwata* range is imported into the UK by *The Airbrush Company* at Lancing near Worthing. Doubly fortunate, I was holidaying within striking distance of Lancing that year and therefore decided to drop in on them in July 2014.

The Airbrush Company was established in 1947 as *Conners Patents Ltd*, producing the legendary *Conopois* (a fixed, double action gravity feed brush that – for its time – created astonishing performance) eventually selling to *Rotring* in 1988 (when I was lucky enough to use a *Conopois* for a limited time).

Following *Rotring*'s decision to pull out of the airbrush market (due in no small part to the rise of computer art), the original owners bought the business back in 1992 (the amazing *Conopois*, however, had ceased production) and import licences for *Iwata* and *Paasche* remained with the business. Now located on the Lancing Business Park, I turned up there on a hot summer day…

Greeted by Lisa Munro, I was introduced to Michael Voss in charge of technical support and repair. Michael listened intently, asking me what I currently used in terms of equipment, what types of paint I preferred and the applications (in this case Art and Modelling), then showed me the entire *Iwata* range as appropriate to my personal requirements, including compressors and accessories (also giving hints and tips on proper care and maintenance – an eye-opener, even for this seasoned airbrusher). After setting up an account with the lovely Ruth, I left with a fairly clear idea of my ultimate set-up.

I had a lot to mull over and over 4 months I crafted and re-crafted my ultimate set-up, placing my final order through Ken Medwell (Director Accounts and Sales), who allowed me to tailor it to perfection. After setting a delivery date (all large orders are final checked by the aforementioned Michael for quality before despatch) two large packages arrived at Cromer Shipyards just before Christmas 2014.

My Set-up

The following set-up covers both modelling and artwork. Some items will not be suitable for the everyday hobbyist. Some, however, will be perfect for those who specialise in certain areas.

All airbrushes need a reliable power source and my compressors have served me well over the years. Unfortunately one of the airbrushes

05: Crown caps bought for the *HP-BH* and the *Kustom K-CS* – well worth the price at under £10 each.
06: The *Kustom K-CS* comes in a very sturdy end-opening box.
07: All *Kustom* range airbrushes come in a brushed metal box.
08: The inside of the *K-CS* box. The brush, wrench, lube and an inline water trap – all as standard for a very good price. My beloved *Talon* now looks like an also-ran in comparison.
09: The *K-CS* in operation. Although it looks cumbersome, it's actually really comfortable in operation. Note the inline quick-release MAC (£20 extra).
10: Close-up of the inline MAC valve. Not suitable for use with the *Custom Micron CM-C* or *Eclipse G5*.

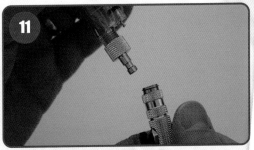

11: The quick release in action – just push to click in, pull the top collar to instantly release.

12: *OHHHH lovely!* The surprisingly awesome *Kustom K-TH.*

13: Inside the brushed steel box. Gun, paint cup, inline water trap, wrench, lube and round pattern cap.

14: Additions bought for the *K-TH*, a larger paint cup and comfort handle extension.

15A: The *K-TH* straight from the box (inline quick-release not included).

15B: The *K-TH* with the comfort handle extension.

16: *Kustom K-TH* in action on a *Starfleet* subject.

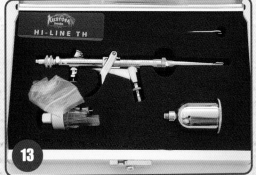

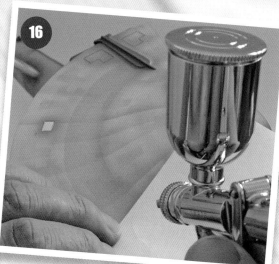

I was purchasing required 1.2CFM (Cubic Feet per Minute) to operate. CFM is not to be confused with psi (Pressure Per Square Inch). CFM is the volume of air that the compressor can deliver to the airbrush during normal operation.

My current compressors, although happy to run up to 60 and 80psi respectively for extended periods, only output 0.75 and 0.9CFM, so a new compressor was needed.

My choice (tested with Michael at *TAC*), was the *Maxx Jet* – one of *Iwata*'s *Studio* series: quiet running, 1/4HP, low maintenance, oilless twin piston with 2.5 litre tank producing 1.4CFM (at 40-60psi) – just what the doctor ordered.

The *Maxx Jet* comes with a 2 x 1/4 BSP outlet manifold (allowing two airbrushes to be used simultaneously), 2 x 3m braided hoses, moisture filter and air regulator. The main compressor is encased in a strong, protective travel case with retractable handle and wheels. There is also storage aplenty, with detachable lid and drawer – all lockable. At £660 it's relatively good value, as my old compressor that only produced 0.9CFM cost me £600 nearly 20 years ago, without half of the features that come with the *Maxx Jet* as standard.

I'm pleased to say the *Maxx Jett* does not

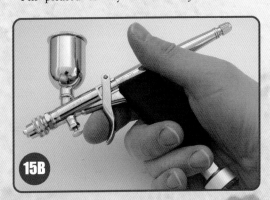

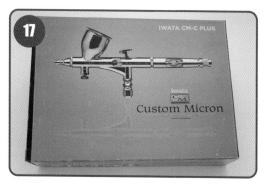

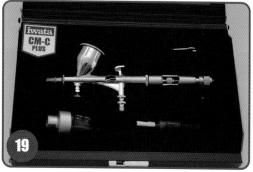

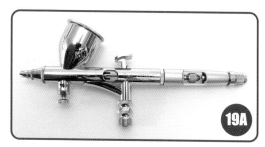

17: Engineering and beauty personified – the *Custom Micron CM-C Plus*.
18: Stylish red enamelled metal box for all *Custom Microns*...
19: ...and on the inside, there's no getting away from it. This level of artistry does not come cheap! Although a wrench is included, I was warned that the nozzle should only ever be removed by a trained *Iwata* technician.
19A: The *CM-C* out of the box.
19B: The *Custom Micron* range comes with crown caps as standard. The second generation now are all fitted with this nifty crown cap dock on the end of the needle limiter.

disappoint, allowing for the flexibility of using airbrushes of all sizes up to a small spraygun without the noise or clumsiness of a large industrial compressor. It has also extended my brush sessions from 30 mins to 1 hr without the need for the compressor to cool – very handy indeed!

If you have the funds for a long-term investment, it comes highly recommended. Unfortunately it's not as quiet as my old compressor but, as it has a larger tank, the slightly increased volume is not really an issue. In addition to the above I also ordered quick-release male and female connections, the female connectors being fitted with inline MAC (Micro Air Control) valves.

The airbrushes

As stated, I was looking to replace all my airbrushes *(with the exception of my Paasche airbrushes and Revell Omega compressor, now relegated to offsite work)*. What follows is a brief overview of each brush and its capabilities. Let's start with the basic set-up I will use for virtually all the review work I do for this publication.

NEO TRN1 gravity feed pistol trigger airbrush

The *NEO* range is the entry level *Iwata* designed for the beginner, and can be used on the smallest of compressors (operating pressure 5 – 35psi). The *TRN-1* is a direct replacement for my ageing *Fengda AB-116A*.

The airbrush has a 0.35mm needle and nozzle set, and comes with 9ml (with lid) and 0.8ml paint cups, pre-set handle and 5 year warranty. Very comfortable and balanced in operation, the *TRN1* is a fixed, double action brush. By squeezing the trigger you first release the air before squeezing harder to control paint flow. The transition point from air to paint is very positive, as is the needle pre-set, allowing excellent control. I was able to produce very consistent spray lines from $1^{1}/_{2}$ to 1/8th inch and even finer when used in conjunction with the inline MAC. PTFE solvent proof packing ensures all paint types (including automotive) can be used. The *TRN1* lists at £130.

Hi-Line HP-BH airbrush

I wept a single tear when I packed my *AB-200* (the *Fengda* copy of this brush) to go to its new owner. It had served me extremely well and had more than paid for its £40 outlay – I was going to miss it dearly! I then plugged in the *HP-BH* and moved from minor to major league instantly!

Fitted with a 0.2mm needle and nozzle (a 0.3 set is also available as an extra), a 1/8oz fixed paint cup cleverly tapered so even the tiniest drop of paint can be used within it, PTFE packing, cutaway pre-set handle and MAC valve, the brush is extremely well balanced (no sudden movements ending with paint everywhere!). I was able to produce a 1 inch spray pattern down to hairline with a crown cap fitted (an optional extra). The fluidity of control, however, meant I hardly touched the pre-set handle, relying on freehand control only – excellent! The lack of overspray is astounding. The *HP-BH* lists at £225 and comes with a 10 year warranty.

The above are my sci-fi and fantasy bread and butter... now let's look at the remaining brushes in the set...

Kustom K-CS

Iwata's *Kustom* range is designed for custom automotive painting, with larger paint cups, taller triggers, pre-set handles and PTFE packing all round. Rugged workhorses aimed at the professional, there are five brushes in the range and I brought two of them, first up being the *Kustom K-CS*.

A *Kustom* version of the *Eclipse CS*, the *K-CS* is fitted with a 0.35mm needle and nozzle set, 1/2oz paint cup with lid and cutaway pre-set handle (10 year warranty and PTFE packing). The airbrush comes in a sturdy metal case with pistol grip moisture filter. I also brought an additional crown cap for closer work.

This brush is, in effect, a monster version of my

Paasche Talon, although build quality is far superior and it can take all types of paint including solvent base types. In operation it's streets ahead of anything I've used before, my well loved *Talon* seeming sluggish and rattly in comparison. Although the idea of a pistol grip moisture trap didn't appeal, I didn't even notice it was present after a while. Two inch to hairline with ease (with the additional help of a crown cap – available separately – and inline MAC). At £170 this brush is excellent value for money (the *Paasche* equivalent is £130) and comes highly recommended.

Kustom K-TH airbrush

No other airbrush on the market compares to the *K-TH* – the only model designed from the start to produce a flat fan spray pattern. Although marketed as an automotive touch-up brush for small jobs, it's far more versatile than this.

Fitted with a 0.5mm needle set and nozzle, 1/2oz removable paint cup, 2 heads (one for round, one for flat fan pattern), PTFE packing, pre-set handle and MAC valve, it comes in a metal case with pistol grip moisture trap, as per the *K-CS*. I also purchased extras in the shape of a *K200* custom grip handle and the larger 3/4oz paint cup.

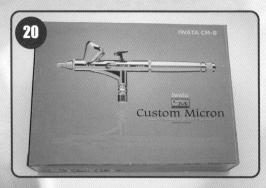

20

21

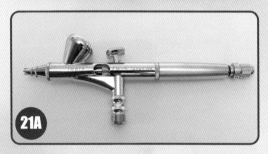

21A

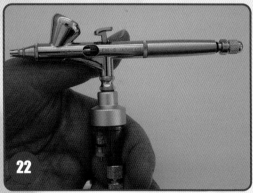

22

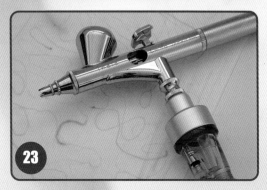

23

The original plan was to use this brush for large scale *Alclad* and *Colour* application. Five minutes in operation, however, designated this brush as my first reach for numerous applications. The fan pattern is excellent and adjustable, producing a fan from 3/4 to 3 inch with virtually no overspray at 60psi. I was also able to produce a tight pattern at 40psi and a fan pattern at 30psi! Switching to the round cap I could spray lines as fine as 1/8th inch (so detail painting on large subjects is not out of its reach) to 3 inch for greater coverage.

The *K-TH i*s an astonishing piece of precision engineering, beautifully balanced and easy to clean in operation. It does, however, require a minimum of 1.2CFM to operate. At £339 it's also not cheap, but for my money is an investment that will pay dividends which I would recommend to any serious artist or model builder.

Custom Micron CM-C (version 2) airbrush

Iwata are world famous for their *Custom Micron* range, which has set the world alight since its introduction and become the benchmark by which all other high-end airbrushes are judged (there are more exacting airbrushes on the market – such as the 0.05mm-headed *Poul* – but these are on the whole individually crafted one-offs and therefore not really within the reach of mere mortals).

Each brush has a machine matched head system and is individually tuned to produce the finest spray characteristics. They come in metal boxes with lube and moisture filter as standard. I bought two of these super machines and intend to use both for fine art and occasional modelling jobs.

The *CM-C version 2* is the latest upgrade on the *Custom Micron* range. As well as the usual machined matched 0.23mm head system, 9ml paint cup with lid, MAC valve, pre-set cut away handle and crown cap, the version 2s now have a taller trigger (as per the *Kustom* range), PTFE seals, redesigned paint cup flow and a clever crown cap dock on the end of the cut out pre-set handle.

In operation the *CM-C* does not disappoint. Balance is perfect, overspray non existent with easy transition from 1 inch to fine hairline, and control is phenomenal. All this does not come cheap, and at £370 (a 0.18mm head set is also available – although this requires a separate CM-C), it's fair to say not every modeller will be buying two or three of these for the toolbox.

However, once you have one, you have a tool which will not need to ever be replaced by a better model (the *Custom Micron* range comes with a 10 year warranty). Can't rate the CM-C highly enough – an excellent tool.

20: The *CM-B* – the finest airbrush I have ever owned.
21: Out of its box the *CM-B* is a thing of beauty. The lack of a MAC is not an issue – it's simply not needed!
22: The *CM-B* hooked up, ready to go. The small size of the *CM-B* is quite a shock when compared to other airbrushes I have used.
23: The *CM-B* in action. This was its first outing and, as you can see in the background, the results speak for themselves.
24: The *Eclipse G5* airbrush.
25: The *G5* out of its box. Even though it's marketed as an airbrush, it is, in essence, a mini spraygun. An excellent one at that!
26: Effective panelling on the *Galor Class Cardassian* warship courtesy of *Iwata*.

Custom Micron CM-B (version 2) airbrush

The CM-B has the same features as the CM-C, except it has no MAC valve (the head set is 0.18mm). The seals are not PTFE (but are

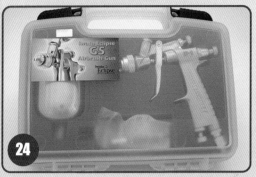

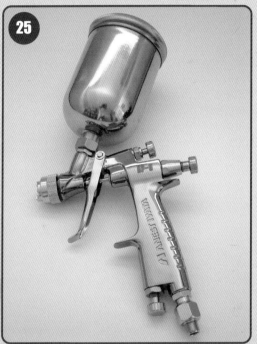

available as an extra, as is the 0.23mm head set), so solvent paints are not to be used. To be fair it's a high end art brush suited for ink, acrylic, water colour and designers gouache.

This is the finest airbrush I've ever used – the fine control is amazing – from a 1-inch spray pattern to ultra-fine line, I can't draw a line finer than what I can achieve easily with this brush. The lack of a MAC valve, although initially a concern, is not missed in the slightest.

Astounding (and at £345, it should be!).

Eclipse G5

This for me is pure indulgence and will only really be used for scenic work, murals and very large models – boy, would this have been handy when building my NebA! Looking more like a small gravity spraygun than an airbrush, the G5 produces high paint flow and relatively good detail in equal measure. Fitted with a stainless steel 0.5 nozzle and needle set, it has a 8oz true centred paint cup (4oz also available), PTFE packing, pre-set needle and MAC valve and comes with a 10 year warranty.

This is a spraygun, pure and simple, requiring a minimum of 1.2CFM to operate. I was able to produce an oval fan spray of 3 down to 1/8th inch very easily. The G5 is a joy to use and very easy to clean – but then it should be as the list price is... wait for it... £475! If you're painting anything over a

meter in size on a regular basis, this is the brush for you.

Conclusions

The airbrushes featured in this review are not free samples sent for evaluation but were bought with hard cash by this reviewer, so if they didn't come up to scratch you would definitely be hearing about it!

For the professional model maker all of the above are highly recommended but for the hobbyist I would recommend some of my selection of *Iwata* airbrushes for the following...

The *Neo TRN-1* is ideal for the every day modeller building the odd model out of the box. If you have the money then the addition of an *HP-BH* would mean you wouldn't need anything else – it's the perfect set up!

The *K-CS* will cover most every day modelling situations (especially with an inline MAC valve and crown cap) and has to be a real contender for the modeller building medium size models on a regular basis.

For the studio scalers out there, if you're going to spend a fortune building expensive kits or crafting huge models from scratch you should seriously consider adding the *Eclipse G5* or *K-TH* along with a *K-CS* to your toolbox as they would pay for themselves tenfold (How much are rattle cans now?).

The *Custom Micron* range is ideal for the figure painter – the *CM-C* for 1/4th to 1/9th scale figures, the *CM-B* for figures from 1/6th to 54mm and below. With the price of some figure kits these days, it would be a foolish figure specialist who didn't consider a *Custom Micron* as a serious investment at some point in the future.

Grateful thanks to Michael, Ruth and especially Ken for their assistance and help in preparing this feature.

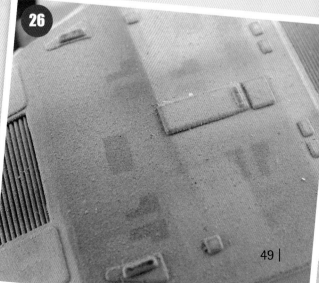

WARNING: BOTH ARMS MUST BE EMPLOYED WHEN FLYING ROUND THE ROOM

Up close with a serious chunk of SHADO hardware, reproduced by Studio 2 Models

Mike Reccia with Bob Smith

SKY 1 IS, OF COURSE, THE ALIEN-ELIMINATING JET FIGHTER THAT FORMS THE BUSINESS END OF SKYDIVER, the iconic futuristic submarine seen in Gerry Anderson's ground-breaking 1970 live action series **UFO**. The largest-scale *SKY 1* studio miniature (around twenty-five inches long, with a twenty-four inch wingspan) happily survived the filming rigours of the series, and has resided in a private collection for some years now, with me being lucky enough at various intervals to have had the opportunity to both study it up close and to also inspect and photograph it at various shows and events. It's a substantial, highly detailed and extremely impressive piece of model-making – light as a feather to enable it to be easily flown on

wires, yet with a menacing bulk and 'presence'.

I've long wanted to reproduce that bulk and presence to the scale of this largest studio miniature, something I can now fortunately do thanks to a recent fibreglass, resin, vacform and plastic kit release by *Studio 2 Models*. Regular readers will be aware that I recently assembled and modified *Studio 2*'s studio scale *SHADO Mobile* over a twelve month period for this title – an extended build time resulting from the pesky intervention of the myriad little surprises life has in store for us, and which get in the way of our true purpose in being here – that being, of course, to make BIG SF models. I had originally intended to

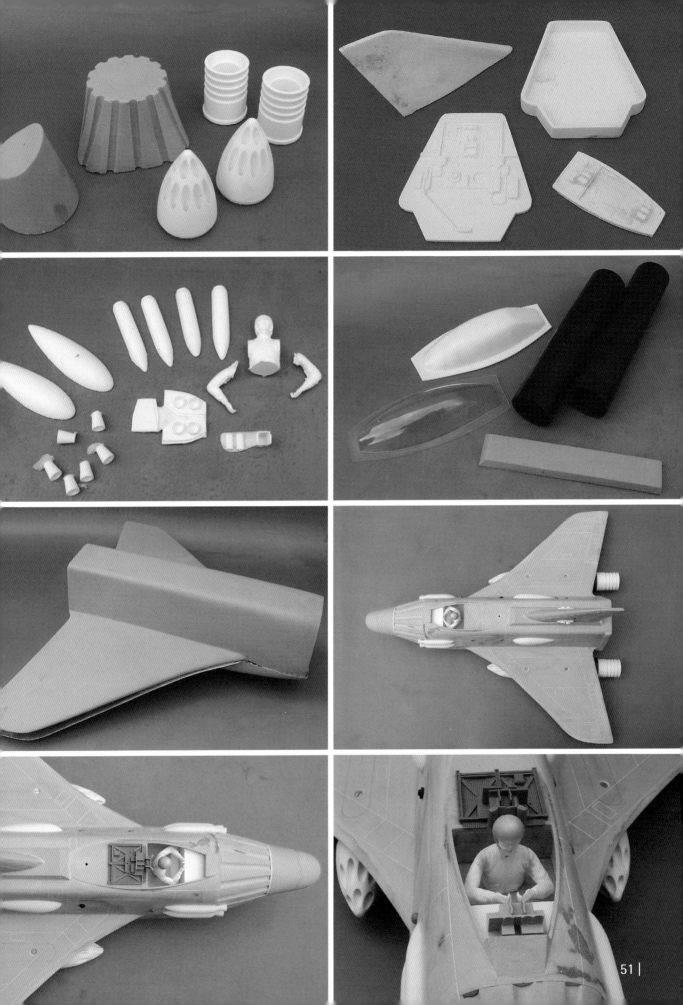

build this new kit and chronicle its assembly in a further multi-part article, but, as I have another *Studio 2* release earmarked for that purpose, I felt you deserved this review as a single 'hit', having patiently trekked beside me during the long haul of the *Mobile* build. In order to review the kit in a self-contained chunk of feature, however, and to do justice in pictures to the treat that this model represents, I would be needing a little help from my friends...

Good mate Bob Smith, whose scratchbuilding, accurising and modelling capabilities put mine in the shade, had also acquired the *SKY 1* kit, and had spent a great deal of time meticulously and precisely putting it together to the point where it was almost ready for paint, so I asked if he would mind me borrowing and photographing it to illustrate this piece. With characteristic generosity, not only did he not mind, but he duly delivered his awesome build to Reccia Towers with the instruction that I should photograph it and

measure it and also take as much time as I needed in doing so – something that would also greatly assist my personal build of the kit. and the amount of time I would need to make the subject (you can't beat having an excellent build available to copy from). In the photographs that accompany these ramblings, therefore, the only shots of my kit are those showing the parts line-up, which is pretty self explanatory.

A modest number of components go to make up this model: body upper and lower halves with integral wings; tailfin base-block; tailfin; rear end cap; rear end cap detailing plate; machine gun pods and nozzles; ridged nose section; nose cap; matra pods; engine exhausts; transparent cockpit blister inner and white plastic cockpit vacform outer; pilot bust and arms; body side tanks and tailfin kit-bash parts, and, completing the lineup, two pieces of plastic tubing for the underwing engine pods. Waterslide decals are also included.

Modellers considering this subject should bear in mind that this is a garage kit, and that above entry-level modelling skills will be needed from the word go in order to put everything together to

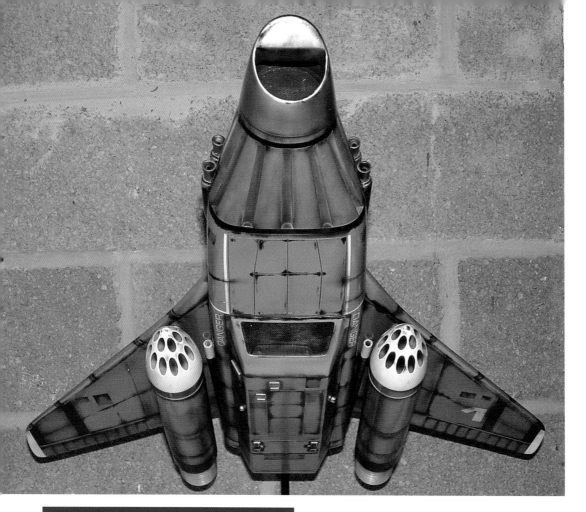

high standard. I have just begun work on my build, so the various requirements of construction, plus any modifications needing to be carried out are being worked out as I go along. In chatting with Bob I am familiar, however, with some of the processes he undertook in assembling and refining his model:

- Redefine tail fin shape.
- Slightly lengthen tailfin base-block.
- Create a raised base for cockpit blister to sit on.
- Strengthen base of cockpit blister to retain integrity of its shape.
- Create a basic cockpit tub and interior (as in the original) and augment this with kit bits (not supplied).
- Cut a hole in the rear of the body and, via this, pour a mixture of resin and filler into the hollow wings to strengthen them (although Bob stresses that this is not absolutely necessary and that the wings on the original are, like the kit's, light and flexible).
- Trim approximately 16mm off the front of the nose section. (NB: *This is not now necessary* as Mamas at *Studio 2* has reconfigured the piece and this section on my kit matches exactly Bob's cut-down version in length.)

- Scribe in all panel lines.
- Cut down the plastic engine tubes to the correct length.
- Resculpt and add filler to the pilot's helmet to more closely resemble the full-size headgear seen on screen.
- Reshape the curve on the leading edges of the wings.

As a final indication of how gob-smackingly good this kit can look once completed, I include some shots supplied by Mamas of his own build. Beginning mine, and having put together and modified an eighteen inch version of *Studio 2*'s *SKY 1* in the past, I have to say that I don't foresee any major challenges in building this kit if you have the prerequisite of some advanced modelling skills and are happy to carefully drill, fill and file. Of note, however, and as mentioned above, is the need for the cockpit blister to be reinforced in order to retain its shape once the part has been cut away from the excess plastic that surrounds it. Its dimensions when released from its supporting sheet spread out at the lower edges, and this distortion needs to be pulled back in. Bob achieved this by sticking the blister onto a piece of *plasticard*, then routing the middle out of this addition to leave a solid piece of plastic across the back third of the blister's new base and an edge along the inner sides and front of the part that hold it to the correct dimensions. It should also be noted that the blister needs to sit against a raised area on the body that is not supplied and will therefore have to be constructed from scratch from filler to conform to the shape of the base of the blister. Without this area to sit on the blister will not seat correctly against the hull of the craft.

Skydiver is a subject close to Mamas' heart and, over many years, he has refined and re-refined his *Sky 1* and *Skydiver* kits to the point where, with a little patience, effort and some solid modelling skills, the modeller can build up these kits into authentic and very impressive replicas of the original studio miniatures. Amazingly this sizeable release, designed to be built as a stand-alone subject as showcased here, has also served as the front end of a mammoth *Skydiver* build by *Mamas*, resulting in a replica some five feet long. ...You'd need a helluva big bathtub to accomodate that one, methinks.

Finally, it should be noted that both Bob and myself are building our kits to replicate the largest *SKY 1* studio miniature, which was not built to link to an in-scale *Diver* section. ...If you wish to replicate the look of one of the other, smaller *SKY* models featured as the front ends of *Skydiver* miniatures as well as in in-flight shots, note that the cockpit window dimensions and certain of the plant-on details will differ from those seen on the larger model. As always, as much reference material as you can lay your hands on is an essential tool in the building of subjects like these.

My verdict on the model? Although only in the early stages of construction with my build, I do have Bob's *SKY 1* in the house at the moment, and I can enthusiastically report that this kit assembles into a jaw-dropping replica that will not only dominate your entire model collection, but also build and tone your biceps, as you'll definitely need both arms to support the subject when you fly it around the room making engine noises.

The *SKY 1* studio scale kit is priced at £400 and is available from http://studio2models.webs.com/ email: studio2models@hotmail.co.uk

The CAR from U.N.C.L.E.

THE 1:25 SCALE CAR KIT AFFAIR
(With special guest star Andy Pearson as 'The Modeller')

As a teenager I thought that **The Man from U.N.C.L.E.** was the ultimate TV show, despite being obliged to watch it in less than ideal circumstances. My enthusiasm was shared by a friend and it was at his house that most of my viewing took place. Due to the profusion of family members similarly engaged, I was obliged to stand whilst being used as a climbing frame by his much younger siblings.

Despite this dedication, the existence of a special spy car totally escaped my notice. In my defence I should add that I didn't see every episode by any means and that the *Piranha* featured in a limited number of these.

This kit is another welcome re-issue from *Round2Models* of the old *AMT* kit with, I understand, some re-tooling of the windows and the rear light strip. Now that information is garnered from one or two websites that also

refer to the new issue as having alternative tinted windows and decals for a track version. Those were not in evidence in the kit I received which, despite being boxed and complete with instructions, was presented as a review copy. By way of extras I received a *ParaGrafix* photo-etch set (see *SF&FM* issue 37) and their decal sheet.

Before battle commenced I ran a visual check over the parts and carried out some very minor clean-up before 'painting' everything with methylated spirit and then applying *Halfords* grey primer to the parts other than the clear and chrome plated ones. I then painted all the relevant body parts using an automotive product from a rattle can. Determining the colour was a matter of judgement as there was no clear guidance available that I could find. An on-line piece referred to a standard *Chevrolet* blue being used originally so I tried to find a visual match. The images of the show's car seemed to suggest a hint of metallic and I eventually chose *Halfords Ford Tonic Blue* which I had seen Mike Reccia use on his **UFO** *SHADO Mobile* and which looked about right. This choice also meant that I could pass any remaining paint to him for use in re-touching – it's never a bad idea to keep in with the management.

The first assembly stage concerned the engine which was made up from twenty-six individual components and went together without any difficulty after the relevant parts were painted in metallic grey and semi-gloss and matt black. Whilst this assembly was set aside to dry I took another look at an area that my test fit had indicated might present a minor problem.

This was the roof and, more specifically, the front pillars that would frame the windscreen. One of these was very slightly out of true and, had this been a resin kit, I would have tried to coax it back into position by softening with warm water. Experience suggested that this wasn't going to be an option with injection-moulded polystyrene so the pillars would have to be glued to the windscreen.

My adhesive of choice for transparencies is *Micro Kristal Klear* but that proved to be insufficiently strong so the alternatives seemed to be either poly cement or superglue. The potential problem with both of these is fogging so I tried several alternative brands using an old canopy from the spares box as a test bed, discovering that *Zap-A-Gap* medium worked best. The *Piranha's* windscreen was duly clamped to the frame and the adhesive applied in tiny amounts. As the tests had indicated, there was no fogging (which I'm inclined to think is more of a problem with enclosed areas such as aircraft canopies) but a spot of glue had worked its way under one of the clamps. This was removed using a combination of new scalpel blade, fine abrasive paper and wadding metal polish.

Whilst I had the roof and windscreen to hand it seemed logical to fit the gull-wing doors using the new photo-etch hinges. These were beautifully engineered but, given their diminutive size and apparent delicacy, I approached them with some trepidation. Having trimmed and folded the first of the four hinges I realised how easy they were to

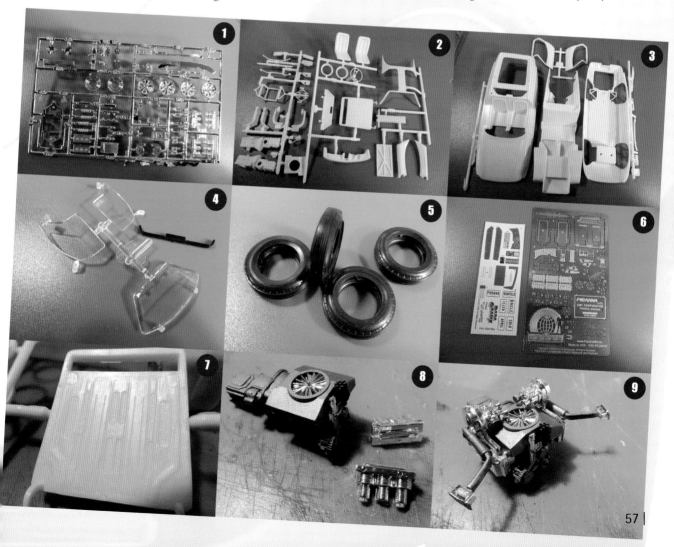

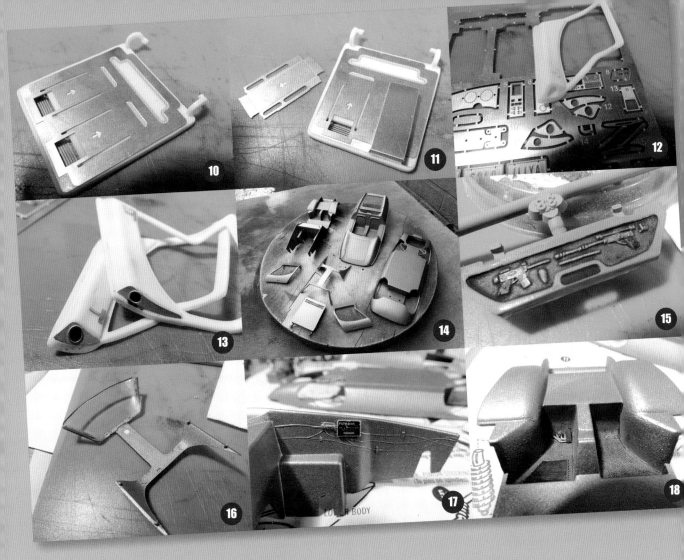

construct although I did use a little surgery to remove four tiny tabs which, on reflection, should probably have been folded if one has the dexterity to do so: I did not.

Positioning the hinges meant that the doors needed to be taped in place but the final result was quite satisfying and further experimentation at this stage seemed to indicate that the door would function as intended using the after-market product. The proof of the proverbial pudding would be presented once the hinges were glued to the doors and, although one came adrift when the doors were finally tested, this was a minor glitch and soon repaired. The doors also feature brass etch openings for the rocket launchers and there are two tiny chromed rockets that can dwell within although I decided not to bother with these. Under the roof is a laser-beam unit (every home should have one) and this needed some simple surgery, described in the after-market instructions, in order to fit round the hinges.

Setting aside the door and roof assembly I continued with stage 2 of the build which consisted of installing the engine, chassis, lower body and the steering and suspension. This was problem-free but, despite having strayed from the prescribed path myself earlier, I would stress the importance of following the order of build indicated in the instructions. I suppose this is stating the obvious but suggest that there is a tendency amongst experienced modellers to work to one's own schedule on occasion, of which more later.

Wheels and tyres were next and I understand, again from on-line sources, that the release kit will have pad-printed tyres featuring the distinctive red pinstripe. It had occurred to me that the chrome wheels might benefit from some weathering in the recesses. To achieve this I brush-painted the recessed areas with semi-gloss clear acrylic and, once this was dry, applied a light coat of *MIG* black pigment powder.

10. Photo-etched panel to rear hatch.
11. Rain cover assembly and fitting.
12. Door with photo-etched extras.
13. Rocket launcher panels.
14. Body with paint.
15. Bulletproof shield and additional weapon detail.
16. Roof frame with windshield.
17. Plaque decal to engine compartment.
18. Cockpit floor detail.

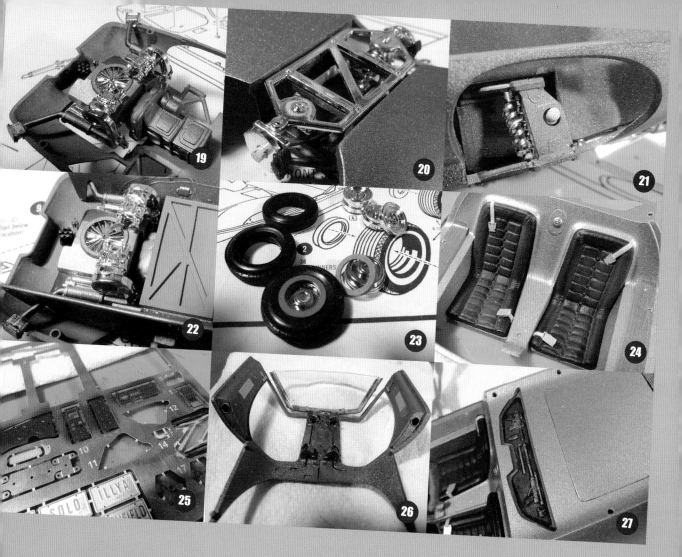

19. Engine in position.

20. Front axle sub-frame and steering.

21. Rear suspension detail.

22. Floor pan fitted.

23. Wheel assembly.

24. Seats with masking tape seatbelts added.

25. Wood effect paint to dashboard details.

26. Photo-etched door hinges.

27. Bulletproof shield in position.

The cockpit benefits considerably from the photo-etch extras which represent foot pedals and instrument panels, the latter having matching decals. These feature some really well rendered wood grain and there are two similarly textured decals that fit on top of the sills under the doors. It would be difficult and, indeed, churlish to criticise the decals but they needed the minimum time in water (literally a dip in and out) and a sealing coat. I experimented with both *Johnson's Pledge* and *Tamiya* semi-gloss clear acrylic, both of which worked well.

An interesting detail on both the kit and the after-market etch set is the central gauge panel which is push-fitted into place as it has two detailed sides, one the standard gauges and the other spy car defensive and communications controls: a nice touch.

Photo-etch fittings for seatbelts were provided and the belts themselves were made from strips of *Tamiya* masking tape.

Having established that the upper body was quite a snug fit during dry runs I thought it wise to fit it at this stage. Before doing so, a hand-weapons panel needed to be fitted behind the seats and the bullet proof shield put in place, either upright (the option I chose) or push-fitted on top of the weapons panel. It's perhaps worth noting that there is no rear window. The rear deck lid also needed to be positioned. The photo-etch set provides a replacement grille for this as well as a new underside to the deck lid and two rain cover boxes, folded from the brass. Not being an automotive engineer I don't know what these are actually for, only that they ain't there anymore.

With these in place (and there's no mistaking their positions) the deck lid couldn't close fully because the rain boxes fouled on the superchargers and carburettors. Now this *must* be something I had got wrong, given the attention to detail with both kit and photo-etch set, but I'm at a loss to know exactly what and the *ParaGrafix* website was down for maintenance at the time so I couldn't shout for help. In the event, the two boxes were removed.

I now welcome you to the standard 'Andy Drops a B****ck' section of this review. Several test-fits of the upper body revealed the best way of fitting it so I decided that, whilst I had my hand in, I might as well glue the thing in place. This I did, aided by several clamps, and set the assembly aside to dry.

The following day and a quick inspection of the remaining parts led me to wonder where the turbo-charger exhausts fitted. The answer was obvious: on either supercharger which were, in turn, now under the upper body. Two hours of surgery using tweezers and a great deal of rough talk finally got these in place and, once they were firmly fixed, I added the chromed exhaust tips, followed by the turbo exhaust doors mounted in the open position.

'Twas now time to fit the roof, door and windscreen assembly, which went in place quite well, although there were still some fit issues with the roof pillars. I had intended to use the *Micro Kristal Klear* product to hold the lower edge of the windscreen to the body but, one again, some extra muscle was needed so out came the superglue. My concern here was that I'd given a black edge to the transparency using a spirit marker and that the glue would disturb this. It did not. I now found that only the passenger door would open – and that after some coaxing with a knife blade and at the cost of a hinge which was glued back relatively easily.

The final parts to be fitted were the rear light transparency, bumper, grille shell, grille bar and fuel filler cap, several of which could (alright *should*) have been fitted before the upper body was glued in place but they went on easily anyway. A minor but slightly annoying problem here was the chromed bumper which was found to have broken in two when removed from the runners. Here I have forensic evidence that this wasn't my fault as some of the chrome plating had migrated into the break. Forward gun barrels were provided

28. Rear hatch hinge detail.
29. Interior roof detail.
30. Coaxing body shell fit #1.
31. Coaxing body shell fit #2.
32. Turbo-charged exhausts...
33. ...and in position. Note that the rain covers have been removed.
34. Grille bar.
35. Propeller shafts with photo-etched detail.
36. Underside of engine compartment.

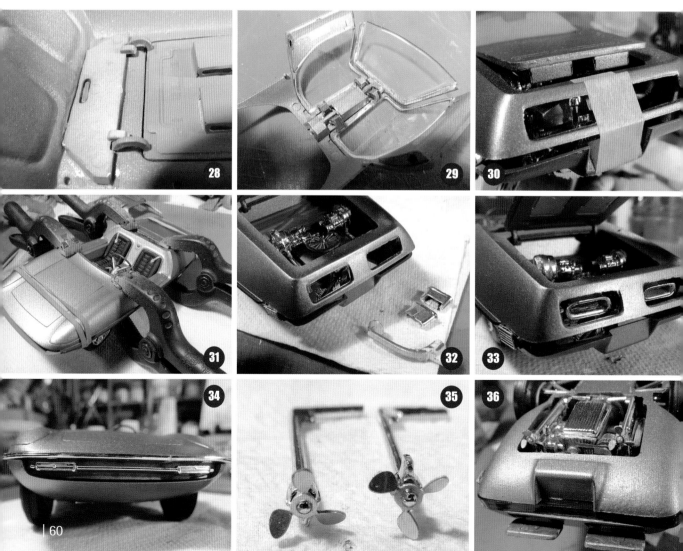

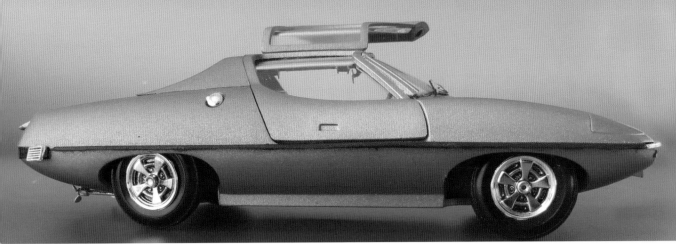

amphibious or at least pretends to be) the license plates and the windscreen wipers. Brass etch plaques and decals provide several options for the license plates and I chose 'U.N.C.L.E.' and 'WINFIELD' in deference to the original car's designer.

The kit's packaging suggests that it's for fourteen years and over and I would add that the after-market photo-etch set perhaps pushes that skill level up a little. Having said that, this is a kit that the experienced model car builder could have all sorts of fun with, especially if he or she followed the correct order of assembly – unlike some people I could mention.

as chromed parts but I think one would have to lose the grille bar if this option was chosen.

The final photo-etch parts to be fitted were the propellers (as the name suggests, the *Piranha* is

Thanks to AMT/Round2Models and ParaGrafix for the review kits.

www.round2models.com
www.paragrafix.biz

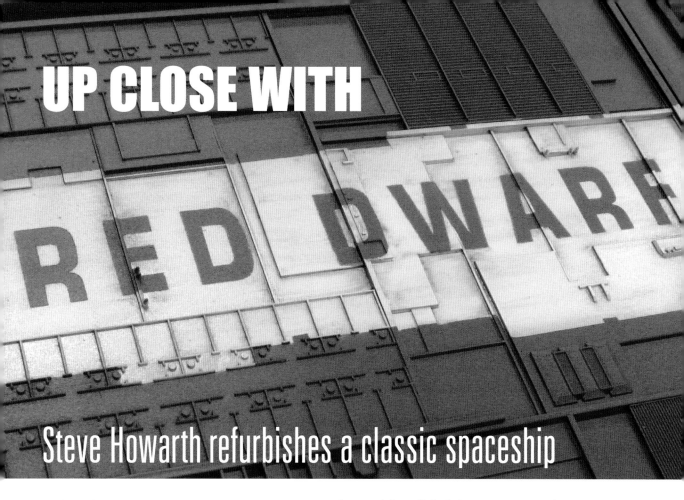

UP CLOSE WITH

Steve Howarth refurbishes a classic spaceship

In 2011 Steve Howarth, with precious little time or budget, was tasked with sprucing up an ageing filming miniature and creating some new additions to the **Red Dwarf** universe. In the following article Steve chronicles his model-making for Season Ten of the popular TV series...

Red Dwarf – the ship

Shed 116D, Shepperton Studios, beckoned once again, working in Bill Pearson's workshop for **Red Dwarf X**...

It's always a buzz to be working at the studios, and even nicer when it's not only science fiction but also working for Bill, with whom I've gained sufficient trust over the years that he more or less leaves me to my own devices.

I felt honoured to be given the task of refurbishing *Red Dwarf* herself. Such an iconic spaceship with a long history and a huge fan-base to make happy... I knew there were a lot of people that would gnaw off their own arms to work on this production, but there wasn't a lot of time for feeling daunted and freaking out, so I piled into things the best I could so as to avoid lingering on the gravity of the situation.

Red Dwarf herself had been in storage for twelve years and wasn't originally made to be filmed with high definition cameras, but this was 2011(?) and 'Big Red' High Definition Cameras were scheduled for the shoot, so *Red Dwarf* needed to be reworked (As you can see from the photos of her condition before the refit). One of the main problems was that *Red Dwarf* wasn't built to be disassemble-able and all the perspex sheets that everything had been stuck to were stuck to each other with lots of superglue, which made getting inside to sort out light leaks with alluminium tape virtually impossible (the worst offending leaks had a pre-sprayed and weathered strip stuck over them externally and I think the CGI boys may have tweaked a few others that I couldn't get to). There were a few screws hidden under wiggets that I *could* find and – I assumed – a lot I couldn't. There really wasn't the time for popping off every lump to look for a screw head that may or may not have been there. Edges were still glued and the perspex was old and brittle, so the plan to leave the basic structure intact was a good one.

Removing and remaking the facets needing it most wasn't an option due to time restrictions, so

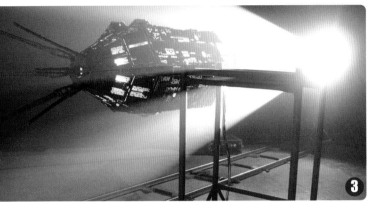

Here are some workshop photos, along with a *few* photos that I took on stage, but there wasn't a lot of time for that, either, as, understandably, there's a film crew buzzing around wanting to get on with the job and that clock that's ticking is very expensive.

1: That large scar was a piece not to be found in the box of bits we had, so I made something else to fit over it ...eventually. 2: That white stuff? Its not *Foamex*, is it? NB. There were no built-in access panels in the main section. The scoop was removable and the engines were removable and that was it! None of the side panels came off – they were all superglued perspex. I could therefore only go in from outside with a chisel/jigsaw/crowbar/whatever. You couldn't even trickle any *Debonder* in there. 3: This was the only way the main ship was shot – on a stand. Lots of photos floating around the internet with it hanging from wires are *not* from **Red Dwarf X**. Because the ship was so heavy, I made the stand longer at the front, so it would never fall over. Freestanding, no scaffolding needed, nor stage weights. 4: You can see where the light leaks are on this still. I think there might have been a little CGI tweaking in post production.

having sides removable wouldn't have helped me here. However, lots of really bad windows had to be scratched off back to the clear perspex and then a new (old) piece scavenged from the chopped midsection (many of you will already know that this stubby pencil used to be a lot longer) could be stuck over the top and the light would still pass through. Some windows were randomly unusable, so a strip of pre-sprayed styrene would be stuck over the top, or a 'wigget'. In an attempt to get away from the even lighting of windows that often makes a model look 'modelley' (like the ones of the *Deep Space Nine* station – nice model, but every window is white!) marker pens had been used in various colours, which had bled over time onto the surrounding area. Some of the marker

would come off with fine grade wire-wool, others had to be covered with a new wigget or an old window panel or a pre-sprayed strip. Unfortunately, towards the deadline, there wasn't much time for me to take lots of close-up pictures of 'after' from these positions. Before and after shots would have been worthwhile doing, but when your mind is focussed on finishing and delivering to the set it's easy to forget about posterity. Suffice it to say, all facets had to be reworked to a greater or lesser degree.

Apart from the black marker, windows had other problems where the previous builders had left scalpel marks as they removed masking tape after spraying. This allowed light leakage and

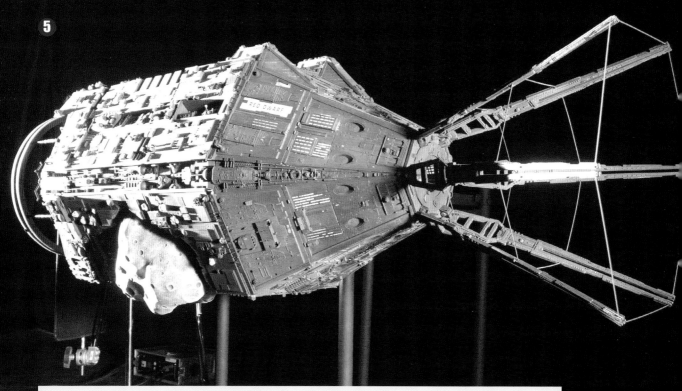

5

5: Basic configuration from the last time is the same but, with an overhaul on all sides, the general feel should be a lot sharper. Having said that, two of the six facets were never filmed. 6: This harsh lighting is a more realistic way of lighting than **Red Dwarf** is used to.

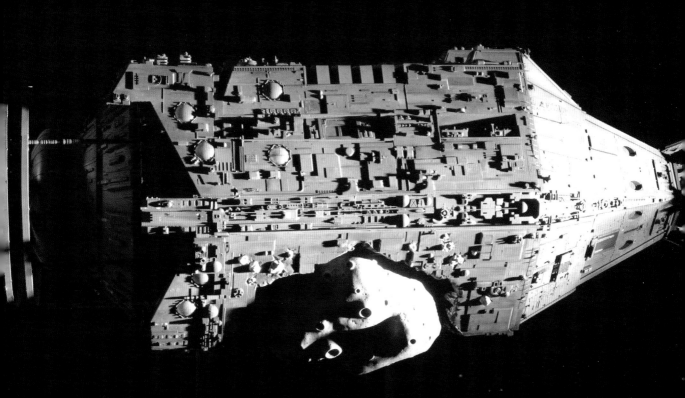

6

7: The downside of the shadows is that they hide all that extra detail I'd placed in the damaged recess. 8: *Red Dwarf* before I really got going on her. She looks alright from here, but if you go in closer (and production intended to) you can see how bad the surface was. 9: A nod to a funny photo someone took of one of the irish crew pretending to cut my *Pachyderm* model from **Space Truckers** in half with a rip saw. 10: Originally, blending in aquarium pumice was tried, but it was going to take too long, be too heavy and there wasn't as much control as starting from scratch. 11: Double checking for blank areas. You can see where I've pencilled in where I think it needs more little craters. 12: A small piece of the old *Dwarf* stuck there just so's it ties in a bit. There wasn't much left that was good enough to use.

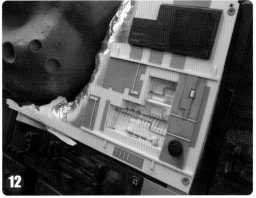

spoiled the line of the window, occurring in a few isolated places but not all, and suggesting that more than one person was involved with the de-mask. Some may have been de-masking much faster than others and so this is not a criticism when a deadline is involved and you know what you can get away with – and twelve years ago they did! Ideally *Red Dwarf* herself should have been rebuilt much bigger for the HD cameras and the windows brass-etched or 3D printed and lots of access panels built in. Doug expressed a desire to do this for series XI, but it's all a case of budget permitting.

13: I can understand what they were trying to achieve by doing this and, although I'm sure it worked from a distance, it doesn't work in close-up. As it happens, the reshoot didn't take us as close as we were led to believe. The places that were good enough to leave alone on the ship were few, but they set the standard and there was no point in going further than that, mainly because there wasn't time and they needed to blend in – not a criticism of the previous model-makers as I don't know how much time they had. 14: The panels' home was an area in much need of replacing, but as not all areas could be cut out, scraping off all the paint back to the original perspex was the answer, to allow for the light to pass through to the (new/old) windows. Three panels in the middle are also from the old ship but not as was. Each was itself made up of pieces and wiggets. 15: ...and after paint... any slight difference in colour was only going to help with the break up of sections and panels and the idea that certain parts of the ship are older than others. 16: Unbolting the engine array so I could stand her up on her end was a no-brainer as far as I could see. It meant I could work on all six facets on my own bench. 17: A close-up of the Asteroid. I researched online for this and the really big ones are a lot like this. There's one the size of Greater Manchester not dissimilar to this. 18: PROOF! Yes, it was me who did the *Red Dwarf* ship refurbish itself.

Lots of stuff wasn't square and so had to be re-stuck or a bigger piece stuck over the top of the scar left behind after I'd chiselled it off (because that's quicker than sticking the original piece back on and making good with the scar and light leaks that are left). Although I don't think time, even twelve years of it, made pieces turn, I'm not judging the model-makers on this. I just think they were stuck on in a rush and looking at some of **Dwarf**'s earlier, jokier incarnations with the crazy dressing, blobs and wot-not, they were probably told not to get too anal with the wiggets as it didn't really matter.

Bigiature

Red Dwarf herself was a bit of an ordeal at times – with lack of access panels and the like. Now I'm not a big fan of interruptions to rythm, but Bill understands the usefulness of a 'sanity break' for

me and so I helped Neil Ellis with what we called the *Bigiature* (big miniature) – a close-up section of the main ship.

Neil Ellis did the lion's share of this job. I just helped out with a few panels and then weathered it as Neil finished off *Blue Midget*.

The *Bigiature* wasn't that big as miniatures go (four feet by twelve feet), representing a fairly small area of the ship in close-up, but with interchangable panels it doubled up as other areas

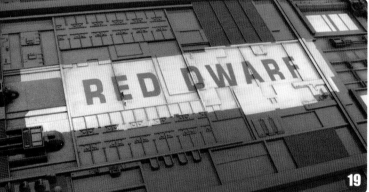

19: The *Bigiature* was a very under-used piece when you know what it was pencilled in for (a long, lingering pass as the credits rolled – more shots of the landing bay – open AND closed) but the logo or name panel was seen quite a bit. Again, not a lot of time or I'd have done some subtle colour changes to indicate different paint strips in the white area (pencil lines would have been too much, methinks). 20: Initially the bay was red like the rest of *Red Dwarf*, but then Doug fancied it in a lighter colour, so it went to grey, which works better when you compare them. Good call, Doug. Shame you never really saw it in the show. 21: I could have painted little paint dribbles below the letters and banded the white more, but there really wasn't the time for that... or, should I say, *the money*. 22: I didn't *just* throw powder paint at it (or myself), but added lots of masking tape so areas would stay clean. I used superfine 0000 gauge steel wool to take back the black before peeling off the tape, then a mist of matt lacquer to seal it all.

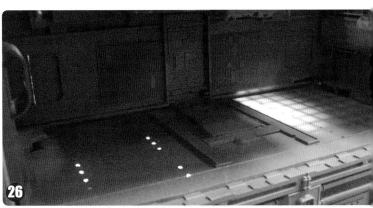

23: Rightly so, Doug wanted *some* windows so it tied in a little with the main model (though it doesn't really match *anywhere* on the ship), but rather than just blank them off with tracing paper/opal perspex and light them, we thought we'd try something else. 24: I knew I had a lot of junk slides in my digs, so I offered to bring them in. *Not* holiday snaps, as Neil jokes on the DVD, but random junk that I'd been meaning to throw away (camera going off accidentally and taking a picture of the roof light...that kind of thing). 25: Idea for the loading bay doors *closed*. Never even filmed. I think they just ran out of time... or they were not needed. It was just another one of the many swap-over panels we made to give Doug more flexibility on the shoot day. 26: Four rows of holes and a torch moved back and forth would have been a nice, low-tech effect. 27: It's not so much which bits I did, but which bits *didn't* I do on the *Bigiature*. The bits I didn't do are not highlighted in green. Not forgetting the swap-over panels for the same areas.

of the ship. (This is certainly not the type of project most laymen think of when you tell them that you're a model-maker.)

So many pieces were used for this that to catalogue them all would have held us back –

creatively speaking – and we know that the fans get a lot of enjoyment trying to figure them all out anyway – don't ask me what they all were, because I can't remember. There were lots of castings from old moulds that I've accumulated through the years from using butchered toys from car boot sales as patterns. Lee Stringer – a friend on *Facebook* – has already duplicated a huge area of this quite accurately.

As with so much of what we do, it's a case of make it up as you go along – there are no drawings – and so there's a lot of fun and excitement as you never quite know how good it's going to be... or even if it's going to be good at all. I was a bit hesitant on this one. Neill opened up more (creatively speaking) and, as a consequence, covered a lot more ground than I did.

The *Trojan* only took a few seconds to stop swaying before filming could begin. Sometimes the camera whizzed by the *Trojan* so closely and so fast it would start the thing moving, as it was only held in place with fishing line.

Fishing lines were either unseen on film or erased by computer graphics in post.

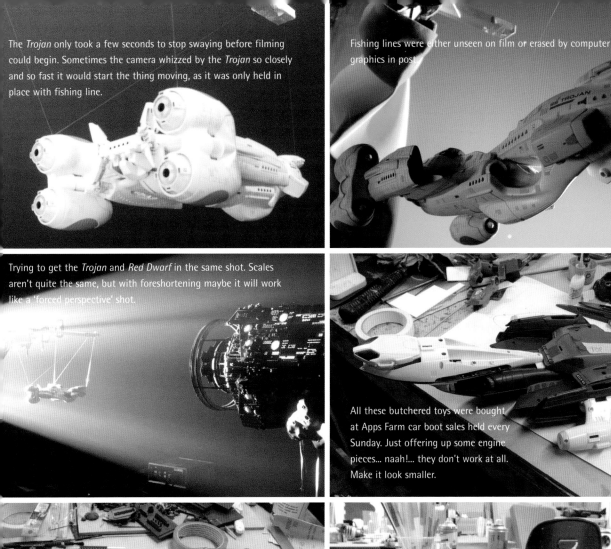

Trying to get the *Trojan* and *Red Dwarf* in the same shot. Scales aren't quite the same, but with foreshortening maybe it will work like a 'forced perspective' shot.

All these butchered toys were bought at Apps Farm car boot sales held every Sunday. Just offering up some engine pieces... naah!... they don't work at all. Make it look smaller.

This was as far as I was going to take the basic shape. Bill said use the toy binoculars Id bought from the car boot sale. In hindsight, it did hide the **Star Wars** toy a lot better than paint alone would have. I'd changed it a bit... but it did need changing more.

Those binoculars might look odd now, but they'll look fine once blended in and painted. Always mindful of the scale, there's a toy car I had nearby as a guide. Works out to about 1:200 scale. The first coat of plastic primer would bring it all together and highlight where it still needed work.

A plot device was to have this clamp around the *Trojan* and then the tractor beam emanate from the front of the clamp. The *Trojan* could also have been composited into the landing bay with the clamp. Sadly, never used. Bill Pearson made the clamp.

With no turnaround time for having brass etchings done (or laser etching or 3D printing) I knifed out the windows from 0.5mm styrene. These tied in with the shape of the windows on the set.

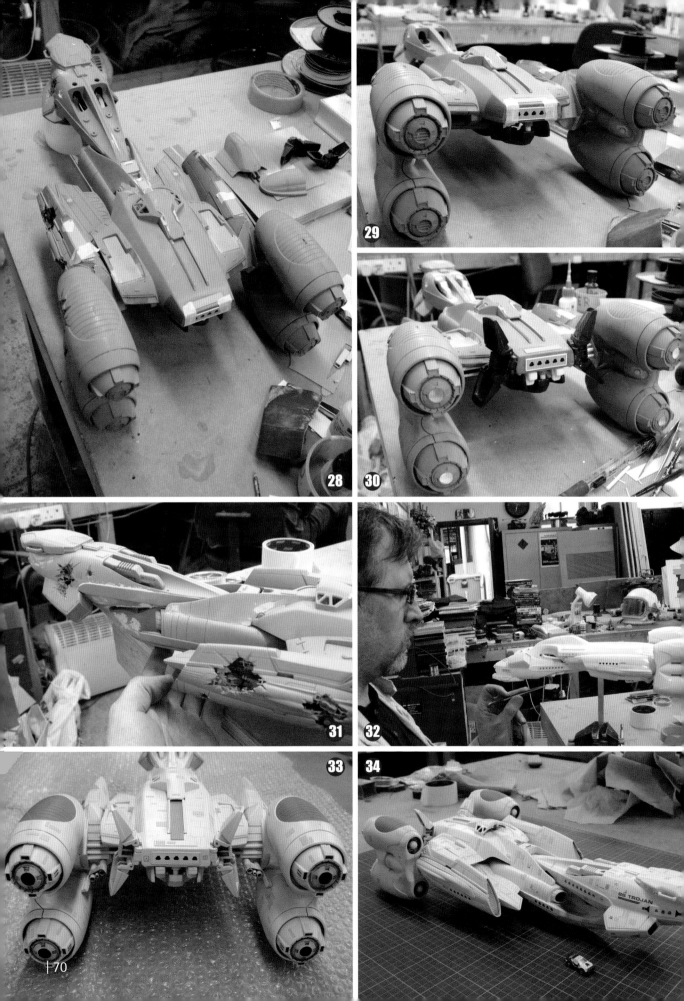

28: Just masking taping the windows in place until their position is finalised. With wiring and lights going in, I need to make as much room inside as possible, so all that filler will have to go. Removed with a *Dremel*. 29: Just like the rear windows on the **TNG** *Enterprise*, I put some windows here as an 'homage' – you can see the 'grain of wheat' bulbs that we used. These give a nice glow and colour temperature but require a lot of power compared to an LED and, as we weren't taking a power line from the *Trojan*, small batteries (and that's all there was room for) meant a limited number of bulbs to give the batteries as long a life as possible. 30: These engine castings go waaay back and came from a Japanese kit I brought back from Los Angeles more than fifteen years ago. We used them on **Space Precinct**! The final colour, as requested by the powers that be. Those fins at the back are the feet from some Japanese robot. 31: You can see Bill's damaged areas that he cut into the *Trojan*. Close-up on the damage and also of a shape used to fix a space bugging me for some time. Part of a toy gun (x2) which Bill donated. I asked him could I have them and he said *yes*. 32: In the vice and easier to get to the underside and panel her up. As the shape went, I think she did have some interesting angles. This is pretty close to an angle used when you see the energy tow-rope. 33: From now on its bubblewrap at all times to prevent any scratching. You can see all the panels on now. I think it was a good call. Doug insisted it needed them and it definitely looks better for it. Luckily, Bill had some *Chartpack* tape, which I was able to pre-cut on the roll and then spray so there wouldn't be cut edges. 34: It's okay to look down onto the model from this angle because we're in the workshop. Guys on stage took our tips (ooh-err) and never did this... always a slight 'up angle' is best, as championed by the late, great Derek Meddings. Whatever it is, it's only got to survive a few hours of shooting on the stage and then it can fall apart – though I'm proud to say none of my models ever have. I always use way too much glue for that to ever happen!

Trojan

The *Trojan* features in the first of the Series Ten episodes. It wasn't a bad little ship for a quick lash-up of various second hand toys, but it did suffer from one major thing... it just wasn't big enough. If I've said it once I've said it many times in this piece, maybe more than I have about anything else, to the point where readers might be getting sick of it, but *there just wasn't any money* and, therefore, *time* to make the *Trojan* from scratch to four feet in length. As it turned out it was about sixteen inches long. (You can see the small car I used to try and keep scale, which was about 1:200, meaning the *Trojan* would have been eighty meters long in reality.)

What could be better than having loose briefs?... I mean *A* loose brief, as follows: Make a funky, fast-looking, streamlined (ish) spaceship and you've got about ten days. Make it up as you go along.

What *could* be better? Well, *designing it* and scratchbuilding it could, but playing around with a pile of junk can also be a lot of fun as you really don't know what it's going to turn out like. Luckily Bill was on hand to give his opinion and stop me from getting too wacky.

35 and 36: Those lights really *did* work. Just never seen in the final cut... or in bonus features. There's always more you could do with a model like this... but you just don't have the time... because someone else doesn't have the money.

As I relied heavily on three or four major toy pieces that I couldn't really stick too much on without it looking like it, I don't feel like I designed this at all and in the truest sense *I didn't* – the guys who designed those toys designed it. All I did was try to blend them together in a way that hid its true nature the best I could. Turning things upside down and back to front always throws people for a while... certainly for the short time it was going to be on the screen. There is one toy in particular from a very famous franchise that I was a little worried about, but so far there have been no repercussions, as only die hard fans have spotted the piece.

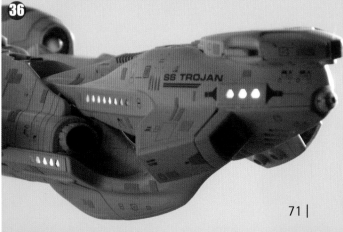

X-WING: GENESIS

In a special photo-feature Senthil Nathan of Shen's Engineering refines the Sovereign Replicas Ralph McQuarrie concept starfighter

SOME OF THE MOST ICONIC SHIPS FROM **STAR WARS** WERE THE *INCOM-T65 X-WING FIGHTERS* that took on the *Death Star...* but before these much-loved starships graced the big screen there existed an earlier version in the shape of Ralph McQuarrie's beautiful concept paintings for the *X-Wing*. Something about its design made me want to build one.

Studio scale modelling has always been a favourite of mine – there's something very special about building detailed models to the same scale as the ones used for filming. All those behind the scenes pictures of *ILM* model makers at work captured my interest at a very young age. They didn't just make models – they created wonderful works of art.

I was therefore elated when *Sovereign Replicas* announced that they were releasing a studio scale resin kit of the *Concept X-Wing* and jumped at the chance to get one. It's a great kit, but I decided on some improvements to make it as close to Ralph McQuarrie's paintings as possible.

The best part of building these kits for me is always the research and the attention to detail needed to make a model more accurate. Finding the right parts from donor kits and the construction has always been a joy – a way of recapturing those special moments of movie magic.

Ralph McQuarrie's art can be viewed at: recklessishe.tumblr.com

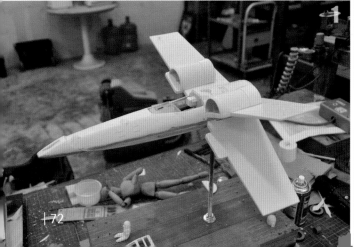

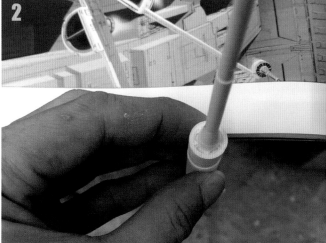

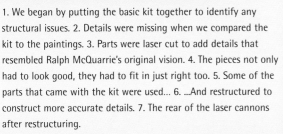

1. We began by putting the basic kit together to identify any structural issues. 2. Details were missing when we compared the kit to the paintings. 3. Parts were laser cut to add details that resembled Ralph McQuarrie's original vision. 4. The pieces not only had to look good, they had to fit in just right too. 5. Some of the parts that came with the kit were used... 6. ...And restructured to construct more accurate details. 7. The rear of the laser cannons after restructuring.

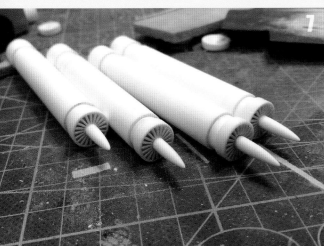

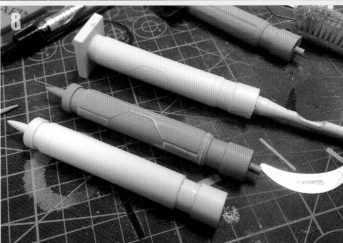

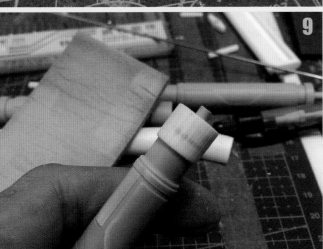

8. The reworked laser cannons compared to the resin cannon (centre) that came with the kit.

9. The forward end of a laser cannon after more detailing and scribing.

10. One of the laser cannons after priming, and ready to receive more work.

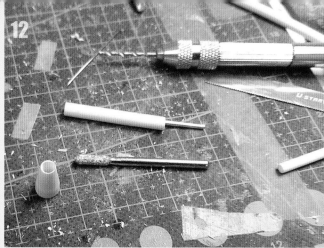

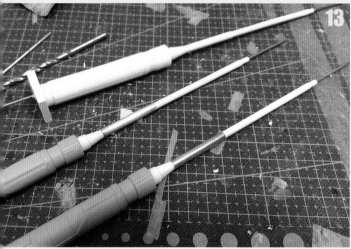

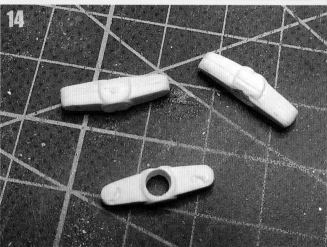

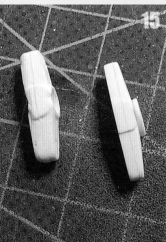

11. The forward part of a laser cannon, just before the barrels were taken apart...

12. ...And refined to accommodate rods and tubings.

13. Brass rods and *Evergreen* tubings were used to reconstruct the laser barrels.

14. More of the parts that came with the kit.

15. New parts were scratchbuilt to replace the resin pieces.

16. A comparison of the part that was scratchbuilt (right) with the one that came with the kit (left).

17. The tip of a laser cannon with the scratchbuilt part and brass tubing in place.

18. The *fusial* engines were also sanded down for the addition of details and panel work.

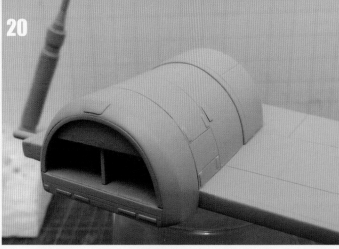

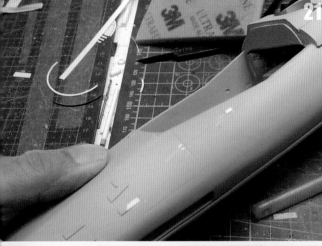

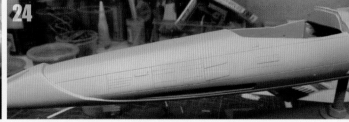

19. The forward half of a partially complete *fusial* engine showing some of the reworked panelling details.

20. An almost complete engine after priming.

21. The fuselage with its cockpit removed. Lots of detailing work yet to be done.

22. The fuselage was sanded down in order to remove its rough finishing.

23. After sanding down, sharper details and panelling lines were added.

24. The fuselage primed and ready.

25. Laser cut details were added to the *fusial* engines after fitting.

26. Parts were kitbashed to add further detailing to the rear of the model.

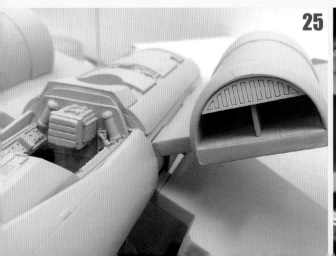

22-INCH ROUND 2 EAGLE ON COURSE FOR LAUNCH

Jamie Hood of Round 2
offers an exclusive look at the year's hottest IP kit

From Round 2's press release on the subject:

" South Bend, IN 6/10/2015 — An all-new, plastic model kit of the *Eagle Transporter* from **Space: 1999** is coming in 2015 to the delight of sci-fi modelers everywhere. Model kit manufacturer *Round 2, LLC.*, an *ITV Studios Global Entertainment* licensee, recently announced plans for the kit at the annual *WonderFest* sci-fi modeling convention held May 30-31, 2015 in Louisville, KY. The officially licensed kit will be the first all-new science fiction based model kit produced under the *MPC* brand in 25 years. It will feature spring-action landing gear and pilot figures with exterior markings included as water-slide decals. It will contain nearly 300 parts in white, gray and clear plastic.

"The precisely detailed model is based on the 'hero' miniature used in Gerry and Sylvia Anderson's television program. At nearly 22" long, it is ½ the size of the original model and is considered to be 1/48 scale. The kit is based on exhaustive research of the original miniature provided by visual effects professional and Space: 1999 model documentarian Chris Trice along with CAD modeler Daniel Prud'homme."

...DESTINED TO BE *THE* THE MOST SOUGHT-AFTER IP KIT OF 2015-16, *ROUND 2'S* UPCOMING 22-INCH SPACE:1999 *EAGLE TRANSPORTER* release has, since the announcement of its imminent arrival via *Wonderfest*, caused sci-fi modellers globally to dream of being able to speed up time. *Don't wish your life away*, they say, but we'd bet real money that many of our readers would willingly trade in a couple of months if they could, in exchange, get their hands on this forthcoming release today

rather than having to wait. Shortly before publication of Volume 39 we spoke to Jamie Hood of *Round 2* regarding progress on this instant classic and asked him to act as tour guide for the exclusive images he kindly provided for this update article...

Jamie explains that the first photographs in this feature picture the *Eagle* mockup unveiled at *Wonderfest*: 'I like to say these mockups are held together by *spit and magic*, but in reality all parts friction-fit together. It almost feels like the parts are held by assembling them while the primer is wet to act as a light glue. In some cases the parts fit tight once we take them apart and reassemble them – in other cases they never stay in place unaided again.

'The mockup arrived with a little damage to the landing gear and some parts have come loose. We used clear tape to hold everything together for the show and you may see evidence of that in the photos. There is a bit of RP artifacting in some surfaces and there are a few other anomalies in a few surfaces that will be taken care of by the time it is ready to tool.'

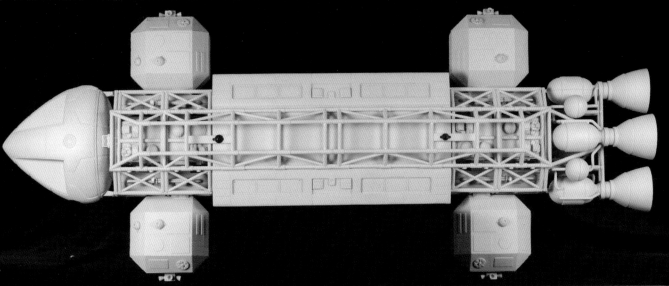

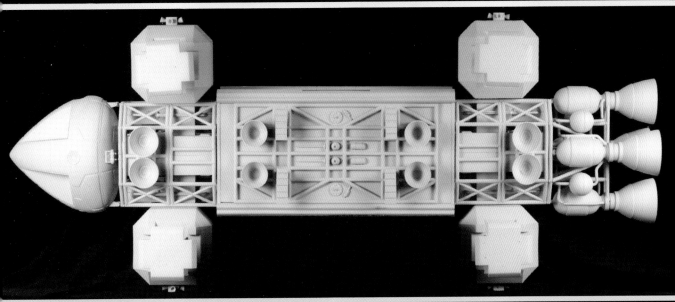

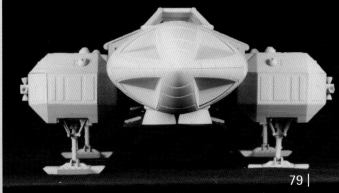

Next we move on to the 'ortho views' provided by Jamie, which: 'show us that the overall look and proportions of the ship are correct. To me one of the focal points of this particular ship is all of the greebly details hidden behind the cages. The overall design is cool, but I feel the 'peek-a-boo' nature of that is really intriguing to the viewer. However, by the nature of the design it is tough to really convey the quality of those details through pictures. I've tried to show some close-ups to show the detail better.

'When we receive digital review files from the factory, we can use them to pull the model apart and examine the interior. Another feature in the files allows us to look at cross section views as well. I'm showing those to give some insight as to how the kit will be parted out, how it fits together and how the innards will work, etc. I'm also showing some screen captures of the inner box details as well as other areas of the ship. A couple wireframe views are shown for the fun of it!'

Lastly, Jamie has included some images of the *Command Module* interior wall: 'This shows the factory's 3D work (again based on *CAD* from Daniel Prud'homme). When we see the test shots, that will be the first time I'll get a first hand look at the real part as no physical mockup of the part was called for due to faith in the digital images and for the sake of saving a few weeks time for RP output and review.

'As of this writing, the tools are being created and I expect test shots in mid-September. Packaging, decals and instructions are all well underway, but none of which can be finalised before we see the first set of test shots.'

One of those test shots is earmarked for this very title, and, if everything goes according to schedule at *Round 2*, this will be reviewed in detail in our next Volume. Stay tuned, *Eagle* fanciers (and that, of course, includes me. Ed.)!

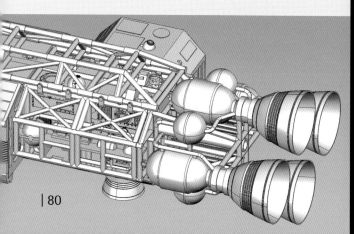

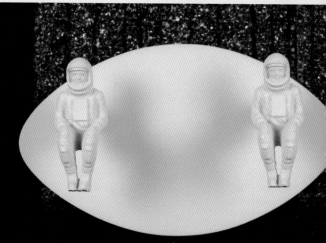

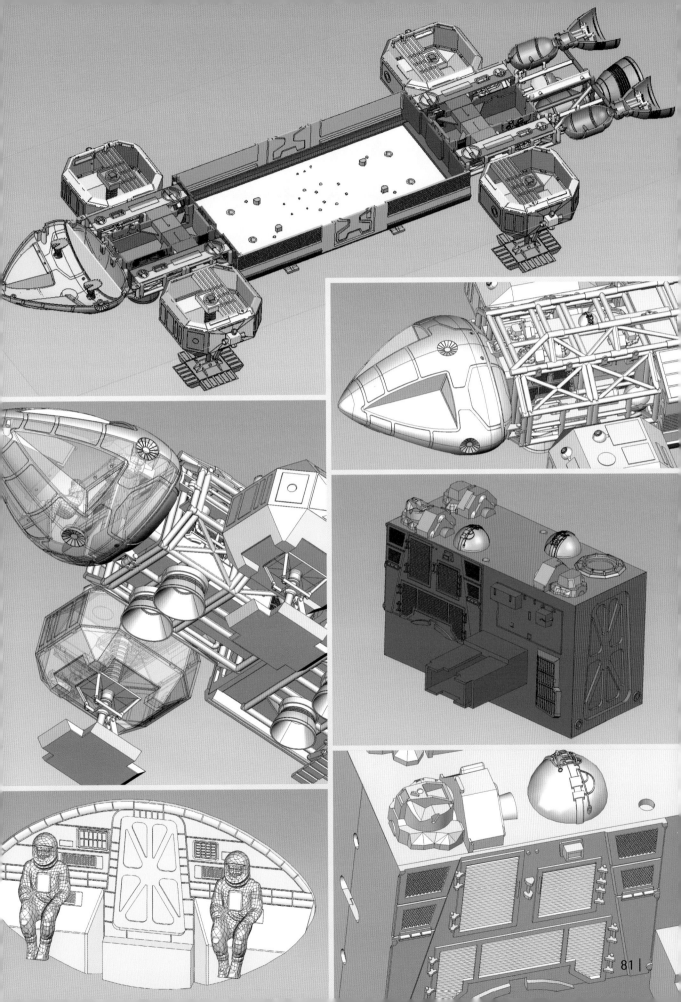

WILD HOUSE MODELS

A flurry of activity from *Wildhouse* this issue, with all new kits being professionally cast by *BLAP! Models*:

Medical Console kit will be finally cast and done together with the doctor sculpt [H] by the time you read this. RRP will be around £85 with doctor figure in 1:24 scale and optional Lighting Kit for additional cost.

Dall Alien Warrior Attacking kit [A-B] is in production now in 1:24 scale. RRP will be £29.95. Kit comes in various options with either the figure being assembled with or without clothing clover and some optional weapons. A standing version will also be available but this has not yet been cast.

Rick Sternbach Warship kit [C-E] is in the final stages of being modelled in CAD ready for 3D printing, with *Wildhouse* aiming at a Christmas/January release. RRP to be confirmed but kit will come with custom decals and optional Lighting Kit for extra cost. Scale will be 1:1400 (around 330mm long) and will include a base.

Pilot Figure: A new figure of a starship Pilot [F] is coming soon in both 1:24 with head/helmet option and one arm either resting on a gun holster or holding his helmet. RRP will be £29.95 and figure will be available November 2015. Also planned is a 1:9 scale version hollowed out for lighting and in a different pose.

A

B

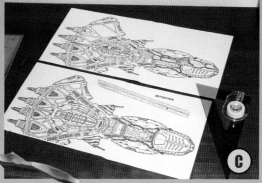

C

D

E

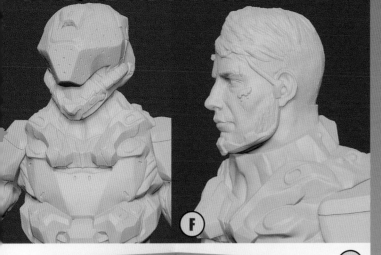

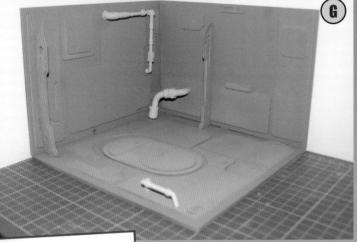

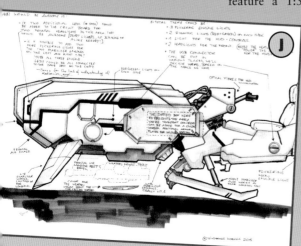

Hobby Zone Large Brushes and Tools Holder
This simple yet very effective holder (easy self assembly) safely stores all kinds of modelling tools – brushes, drill bits, files, pincers, pipettes, etc. Holes of various diameters allow storage of tools of different sizes, plus there's a niche for rulers, large scalpels and other accessories and a bar for hanging scissors and wire-cutters, etc. on. Holder priced at £14.50 from store.modelkitworld.com

also generic enough for modellers to use on any scifi kit or kitbash/scratchbuild, with *Wildhouse* also planning to sell these separately.

SciFi Scenery Boards – Lasercut *MDF* boards for modellers building *Wildhouse* kits or simply for generic scifi scenes needing a diorama. The first set of boards is available now with RRP being £15-20.00 and featuring some of *Wldhouse*'s custom pipes [G] and other materials. 35-40 easy to assemble parts per pack.

ORCA HoverBike kit and Rider: This 1:32 scale kit [J] and *Rider* will be on the casting bench as you read this for a November release. RRP still TBC but expected to be around £85. Will feature a 1:32 *Rider* and optional Lighting Kit and custom decals.

Decals: A new set of decals for the *Hover Bike* but

Mining Ship – 1:350 scale kit around 180mm long. Model is complete but not yet 3D printed. No ETA on this yet as *Wildhouse* are prioritising the warship first so a guesstimate is first quarter 2016. RRP TBC but kit will feature custom decals and optional Lighting Kit as an extra add-on.

Generic Lighting Board for models – A new generic Lighting Kit for modellers. The boards can be linked together and are 37 x 29 x 18mm in size running from a 12v dc power and can power up to 25 LEDs each with 3 inputs. The basic board will have some pre-programmed effects for engines and lights, etc, but other boards can be added for more custom effects using standard connectors so the modeller need not to worry about soldering!

Accessories: *Barrels, Weapon Rack & Guns, Stackable Weapons Crate, Cargo Container, Portable Generator, Gas Cylinders, Backup UPS Power Unit and Medical Boxes.* All in 1:24, 1:32, 1:48 and 1:72 scale. These have been 3D Printed but not yet cast. ETA is end of the year – RRP TBC but they will be in the £9-15 range.

MIKE TRIM GENERATED SOME SUPERB DESIGNS FOR THE HARDWARE FEATURED IN GERRY ANDERSON'S 1967 CAPTAIN SCARLET AND THE MYSTERONS (and yes, I *am*, unfortunately, old enough to remember the unabridged series title). With Derek Meddings contributing *Cloudbase*, the *Angel Aircraft* and the iconic *Spectrum Pursuit Vehicle*, Mike originated the equally memorable *Spectrum Saloon Car*, *Spectrum Helicopter*, *Maximum Security Vehicle* and the *Spectrum Passenger Jet*.

Even more impressive than this last is Mike's original concept sketch for the 'SPJ', which featured underwing pods and sloping, angled wings. The simplified version of the *Passenger Jet* seen on screen is nevertheless a triumph of futuristic design, with forward swept wings, tail fin and stabilising fins building on the design aesthetic established with *Thunderbird 2,* and it is these lines that have been faithfully reproduced in a new resin kit of the aircraft by *UNCL*.

Some twenty inches long, the craft is depicted in in-flight, undercarriage-up mode, this probably due to the fact that the spindly undercart the onscreen version sported would not be able to support the weight of this resin replica, and the kit features a choice of transparent or opaque cockpit canopies (courtesy of vacform or resin parts), providing seats and a basic interior if the former option is preferred. The in-flight configuration does pose a minor challenge, however, in that no pilot figures are provided, an omission which, unless you intend to build a Mysteronised version, will need to be remedied.

Basic construction
As with all *UNCL* kits, parts are beautifully cast with little flash, making construction a very straightforward affair, with only a few pouring lugs to remove and minimal tidy-up of parts, and with all components assembling easily. Some filler was needed around the wing roots and in the join between tail fin and main fuselage, and I chose to pin the front stabilising fins in place to strengthen the joins. Other than that basic assembly took place quickly and easily.

The search for Scarlet
From the size of the three pairs of double seats provided, the jet appears to be roughly 1/72 in scale. A trawl through the spares box for appropriately scaled figures proved fruitless, and an appeal duly went out to Andy Pearson,

Executive Travel for Spectrum's Finest

Mike Reccia builds the SPJ kit from UNCL

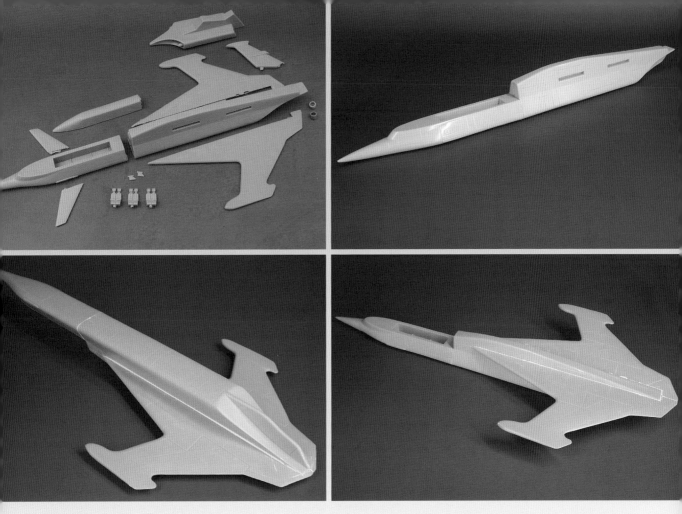

Top left: resin parts line-up.

Top right: fuselage halves joined.

Above left and right: underside and top view of wings in place with joints filled.

esteemed scribe of this very title, who quickly and very kindly sent me a blister pack of beautifully detailed OO-scale *Bachmann Branch-Line 1950s Train Crew* figures. At first the two sitting versions included looked perfect, right down to their peaked caps. Offering them up to the seats, however, I discovered that they were a little on the small side, and would have had to sit on scratchbuilt cushions to reach the controls had I used them. I therefore dove in for another mental swim around the think tank – and suddenly remembered that I had an old cannibalised *Airfix* 1/72 scale bomber kit lurking in the cellar somewhere. Bringing this out to blink nervously in the daylight I rummaged through its contents and discovered a crew of three perfectly scaled figures in flight helmets and breathing gear and with separate, positionable arms.

Selecting two of these I set to work with scalpel and files, hacking away at their helmets, respirators and the mouldings on their chest areas and flattening and rounding off the tops of their heads to create some semblance of the *Spectrum* caps. The figures were then primed and painted up in *Spectrum* colours – one as *Captain Scarlet* and

the other as *Colonel White*, my original intention being to recreate the cockpit lineup from the episode *Flight To Atlantica*, with *Scarlet* in the left hand seat and *Colonel White* on the right. My converted figures were never going to win any beauty contests, and at that scale I found it impossible to add peaks to the caps (they're transparent on the puppet uniforms anyway, so it didn't really matter), but, once installed side by side, I felt confident they would look the part (more on this later).

Cockpit capers

The cockpit canopy vacform and the cockpit interior are the most complex and challenging aspects of this kit. The three sets of double seats locate into a moulded-in cockpit tub and these were primed then brush painted a light blue with silver frames to match what is seen on screen in the puppet-sized set. Over the canopy tub locates a delicate interior framework piece with a central bulkhead and an integral control console at its front. The entire framework was primed in light grey and then matt white was misted over this to lighten the colour. The instrument binnacle was picked out in matt black and decals from the

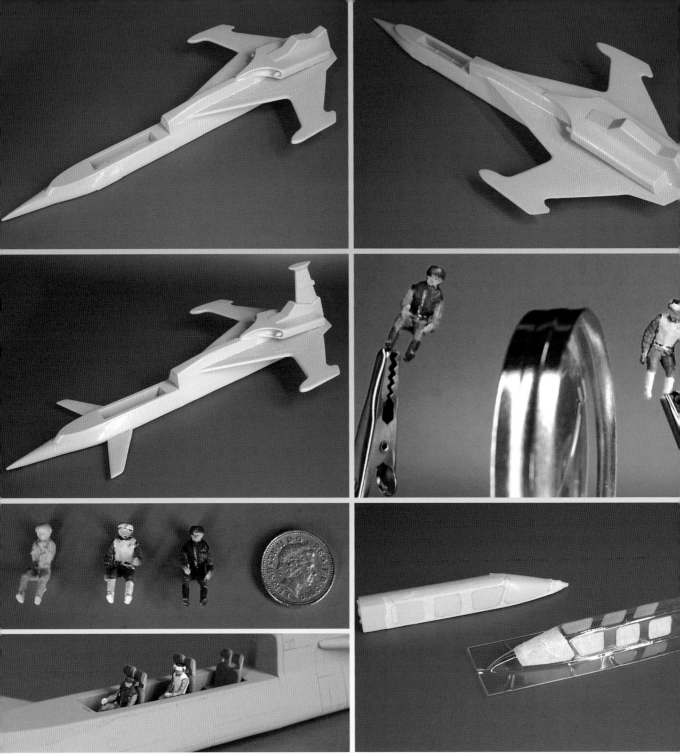

spares box were applied to the control surface to represent dials and gauges. To add detail to the bulkhead I applied a door section front and rear made from adhesive paper label painted the same blue as the seats, framed by a few appropriate decals to represent control panels.

Helpfully the positions of the front and side windows are indented into the canopy vacform and also into the solid canopy option. It is suggested in the instructions that the solid piece be used to help create window masks for the transparent piece, and this proved to be a very useful procedure. Positioning strips of masking tape over the window areas on the solid canopy I was able to trace out the depressions that constituted the outer edges of the windows with a sharp pencil. It was then simply a matter of running a scalpel blade along the lines of each drawn out window frame, peeling back the resulting shape from the solid canopy and applying these over the corresponding window

Top left and right: engine block in place.
Centre left: stabilising fins pinned in situ.
Centre right and above left: from bomber pilots to *Scarlet* and *White*.

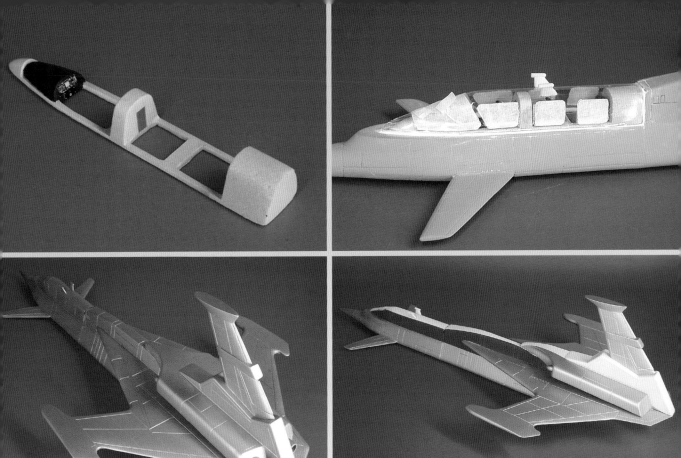

areas on the vacform piece. Using this method it took less than an hour to mask off all the windows on the transparent canopy – splendid idea, *UNCL*!

It is recommended in the instructions that the canopy framework be glued into the vacform cockpit blister part before removing this from its backing and, having dealt with vacform cockpits on many occasions, I can understand why this move is an essential one... once vacform blisters are removed from their backing they lose much of their rigidity and their base contours spread out, making it difficult to reconfigure them and locate them correctly. Test fitting the frame into the blister, however, it became apparent that the two pieces weren't quite a perfect fit, the frame's dimensions being slightly smaller than those of the canopy interior. I therefore, and in order not to cut too much off the canopy when removing it from its backing, applied two-part epoxy to the sides of the frame then stood it on a flat surface, sitting the canopy over it until the glue had set and thus ensuring that the frame's lowest dimension sat

flush with the corresponding lowest dimension of the canopy piece (I hope all that waffle makes sense!).

I duly trimmed the canopy to correct size, but before I could fit it it was time to glue the figures in position, side by side, onto the front seats... or, rather, it wasn't, as I discovered there wasn't quite enough room to sit two 1/72nd scale figures next to each other on the seats. My *Flight To Atlantica* configuration was therefore abandoned and I was

forced to accommodate *Colonel White* in a rear compartment rather than up front next to *Scarlet* – no great loss as it turned out, as a second figure glimpsed further back in the jet added weight to the sense of scale.

The canopy was now secured to the fuselage using two-part epoxy as superglue would have fogged the transparency, and the resulting slight gap between canopy and fuselage was filled and sanded smooth.

A spectrum of colours
Truly sorry for the awful pun... in all seriousness the *SPJ* sports the most complex Anderson colour scheme I've had to recreate since I put together a *Stingray* model several years ago. I began by coating the aircraft in *Humbrol Light Grey Primer*. I then spayed the whole jet in *Hycote Renault Silver Grey* (again, the instructions recommend a silver with some black added to it rather than the bright silver many *SPJ* replicas are traditionally painted in – and I concur with this choice absolutely as reference shots show the jet to have a slightly silver-grey sheen rather than the more toy-like bright silver).

Allowing the silver to dry for a day I next set about masking off the wings, lower fuselage and tail fin so that I could apply the blue. For this I chose *Hycote Ford Maritime Blue* – reference colours vary wildly and this seemed to match the majority of shots rather than the much lighter blue seen in some stills, which I feel is probably a result of harsh studio lighting.

Finally, after allowing the blue to dry for a day, I masked off the complex curving section that runs along the top of the jet, plus the blocky base of the tail fin and the slim fin section to the underside of the craft and sprayed these in *Humbrol Matt White*. With all three colours in place, and with a coat of *Games Workshop Satin Purity Seal* sprayed on to unify, seal and dull the bright finish down slightly, I could finally peel off the window masks and was much relieved to find there had been no creep or bleed of paint beneath them.

Readying for take-off
The *SPJ* sports a plethora of drawn-on panel lines across all its surfaces, and these have been faithfully reproduced as scribed lines on the kit. I drew within each of these with a sharp pencil, doubling up on the mid-wing lines that effectively

This page: the completed model.

separate each wing into two sections to deepen the amount of shadow. In the first **Captain Scarlet** annual this wing split is explained as a deliberate feature intended to allow the outer wing sections to pivot upwards and act as air brakes. Indeed, in reference shots of one of the actual studio miniatures a gap can be seen between the two sections of wing, suggesting that this may actually have been a feature that was designed into the models and intended for use should a script call for it, but which was never actually deployed on screen.

The next step was to reproduce the bright red coach lines featured on the wings top and bottom, on the wing trailing edges topside, on the front fin leading edges top and bottom, and around the base of the cockpit canopy, plus the fat red band that girdles the jet just forward of its wings. These are not provided as decals, and were therefore reproduced courtesy of some red adhesive vinyl striping, with the central band being created by spraying a section of white adhesive paper label with red paint then cutting out and positioning a suitably sized strip.

With the panel lines and red stripes in place a further coat of *Games Workshop Satin Purity Seal*

was applied. The final step was to add the twin jet exhaust pieces (primed and painted aluminium) to the rear of the engine block and the superbly reproduced *Spectrum* roundels to the jet sides and wings top and bottom. These really are beautifully done, the central 'S' gleaming in a gold finish. I decided not to overspray these with the *Purity Seal* as I didn't want to dull their bright colours.

And that was it, paint – and detail-wise – *done*. The studio miniatures featured little to no weathering, the *SPJ* always appearing clean in the sequences that featured it.

Conclusion

As usual with *UNCL* releases, the kit is very well cast and well presented, and the *SPJ* makes a welcome addition to *UNCL*'s other **Scarlet** releases. A highly recommended subject for **all** *Supermarionation* modellers.

Review kit kindly supplied by Timeless Hobbies.

Kit available from Timeless Hobbies. Tel: 07908 295301 Monday–Friday 9am–6pm or email: sales@timeless-hobbies.com

ATTACK
OF THE
SPIDER

Part 1

*Diego Cuenca
scratchbuilds a
Sci–fi Soviet Walker*

Diego Cuenca's stunning scratchbuild of a Soviet Walker in a winter forest setting recently earned him a gold medal and best sci-fi model award at Spain's Leganes 2015 model contest, a silver medal in the Torrent 2015 model contest and a further gold in the Zaragoza 2015 model event. In the following feature Diego describes how he created the menacing star of his atmospheric diorama – the Machinen Krieger-resque 'Spider'...

Concept

How does one go about imagining and then creating so large a piece? Initially I had absolutely no idea, although the first thought that came into my head was to use a battery charger (which became the base of the turret structure). I then considered that, if I added a couple of feet, I could create a *Maschinen Krieger* type of vehicle. After contemplating the dimensions of the *Spider's* large head for a while I felt the vehicle would look better with four legs and began to seriously develop the idea.

Right from the first sketch [1] I'd decided the *Walker* should be Soviet in origin, and should include various characteristic features seen on WWII or cold war Soviet tanks. Additionally I had several items in my house that I wanted to reuse and incorporate into the build, such as the aluminum RB barrel of a *JS-2* and many left-over parts from *Trumpeter Chinese Type 89* rocket launcher kits.

Bearing in mind all these parts I wanted to use, my wish list of characteristics for the 'real' vehicle finalised as follows:

- It should be a Soviet *Walker* with four legs.
- It should have a large, rotating turret with a main gun and a secondary element.
- It should feature radar, anti-aircraft elements and rocket launchers.
- The engine block should be easily removable for replacement in the battlefield.
- It needed a fuel tank and hydraulic oil tank for the leg mechanism.
- Room for the crew in both the body and the turret was essential.
- Various types of shield were required on the body, in the turret and on the legs.
- Hydraulic hoses should be protected if possible.

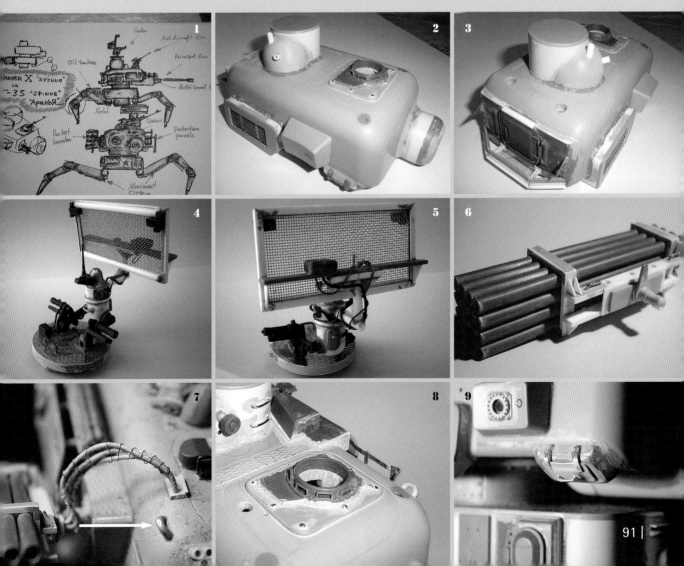

• The 'real thing' would be constructed from a variety of materials such as cast iron (*JS-2*) and rolled steel.

Turret

I decided to cover the battery charger with different structures to transform it into a turret. First I closed off the bottom area with PVC and added the side protuberances where there are vents (from PVC and *Evergreen*). These grids are, in reality, filters used to purify plants in swimming pools.

After filling the charger's four screw holes with putty I added the cylinder that would support the radar (the blue sphere is a *Kinder* egg) plus a hatch from a *type 89* kit. To the rear I attached a section of *type 89* kit which incorporates a hatch. I created a small structure from *Evergreen* profiles and gratings to carry supplies and made the support for the rocket launcher from a computer keyboard key. The barrel support is composed of three parts: the central piece is a section of PVC electrical conduit; the rear is part of a *Kinder* egg, and the front is a porcelain drawer handle fused to a PVC

pipe with putty. This is fixed to the battery charger box with a screw which leads into its centre, and the top of the hole for this is where I anchored the gun barrel.

After adding a shipping container on top of the turret I started to work with the radar. This consists of different types of materials and a great deal of improvisation was employed in its creation. It features parts from the *type 89* kit, plus PVC pipe, tin foil, *Evergreen* profiles and sheets, copper wire and lead, metal mesh and further pieces such as the copper cap, which in reality is used as a plug to seal gas pipes [2-3].

Weld seams on the radar [4-5], as on the rest of the model, were made from *Citadel* putty. The methodology was the same throughout: make a thin putty strip (fingers and tools first covered with talcum), glue onto the area with *Tamiya* glue (green cap) and finally, with a modelling burr (anything with a thin, rounded tip is OK) mark the weld lines and remove any excess. As a final protection, glue was reapplied over the putty.

As guards for the side air outlets I used 1mm thick PVC sheet, cut with rounded corners then bent to give it a subtle curve. To achieve the

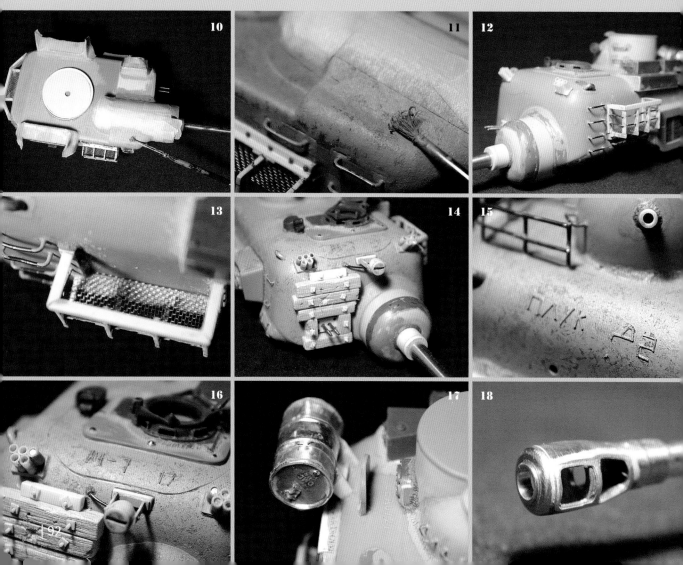

curvature I rested the PVC sheet on a cylinder and pressed it down while I applied a little heat with a hairdryer. The anchors on these turret guards were made from plastic rod, and the rivets are pins passed through the PVC and introduced through the plastic tubes to the turret (these are filled with cyanoacrylate).

The rocket launchers are part of the *type 89* kit, the support structures being made from *Evergreen* profiles, PVC and copper wire. For connection cables I wrapped three pieces of lead wire with masking tape then rolled copper wire onto them.

The turret also has an emergency exit in a low area, this hatch being formed from plastic, two types of putty and copper wire.

According to my initial idea, the turret on 'the real thing' would be made of cast iron, as they were on Soviet tanks, so I applied a generous layer of *Tamiya* putty with an old, worn brush. I then tapped with the brush to get the texture of the cast iron, applying this texturing in several layers until I was happy with the result. Some elements of the turret would not be made from cast iron (such as the structure that supports the barrel and the side

air vents), and these were protected with masking tape as I applied texture to the 'cast iron' components. Also, in some areas on the top I placed pieces of tin foil textured to look like a non-slip floor covering. To achieve this I simply rubbed a piece of tin foil positioned over several strips of plastic packing tape with a dull burnishing element.

As an anti-aircraft gun I used one from a *type 89* kit with some modification to allow it to be anchored to the hatch.

On one side I included a basket for supplies of the type that *Merkava* carries (this element and the outputs of the exhaust pipes are the only two references to non-Soviet battle tanks). The main structure was made of plastic sheet and copper wire.

To both the turret and the body I secured lifting eyes in case of system failure. These are made from tin wire [7] and are approximately 2.5mm in diameter. I also positioned footholds to access the top of the turret and vegetation as camouflage, both made from copper wire of different diameters.

The gun shield was formed from tubes and

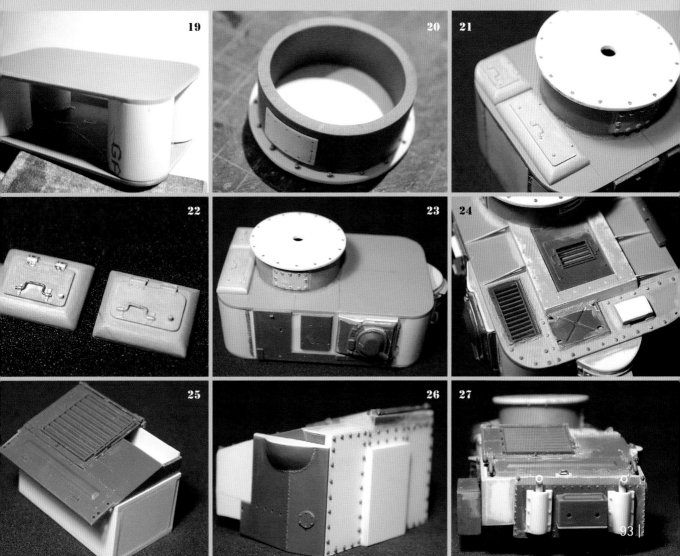

plastic sheeting which were attached to the handle with *Citadel* putty, this simulating a weld bead. The cannon is the *JS-2* from *RB*.

As a coaxial weapon I used a German machine gun *MG* from *RB*, leaving half its length inside the turret. The guns are connected to the turret via a rectangular piece of plastic with four rivets made of stiff plastic. On this front section I wanted to do something even more extravagant ...something made on the battlefield. As a result I anchored a few pieces of wood to the turret with steel rods [14]. In this area I also added a light fitting made with *Evergreen*.

Another distinctive feature of Soviet tanks is their welded-on identification numerals [15-17]. I studied several photographs of a *JS-2* in order to replicate the characters, creating these for both the turret and the body from stretched plastic. *Tamiya* glue (green cap) melted the plastic [9], allowing it to be adapted to the shape of the turret. I then applied the texture over the symbols with putty.

A further characteristic of Soviet tanks is the fuel drums at the rear of the body, here placed at the rear of the turret, with these being made from tin sheet.

Body and engine block

The base of the body is made from four sections of PVC plastic conduit [19] of the type used to accommodate electrical cables, with two 2mm thick PVC sheets for the top and bottom. After gluing the base structure I covered the sides with *Evergreen*. In the joints I added *Citadel* putty to look like weld seams. The next step was the most fun in the entire project – the covering of this structure with parts from other kits and scratchbuilt elements.

For the connection between the turret and the barge I built a mechanism similar to that featured on any excavator using PVC tube and plastic card [20]. I placed the other part of the mechanism in the turret, this allowing rotation and engagement of the two sections without the need for glue – essential at painting stage.

At the rear of the body I wanted to feature fuel and hydraulics tanks, similar in this case to those carried by the *SU-85* tank destroyer. I tried two

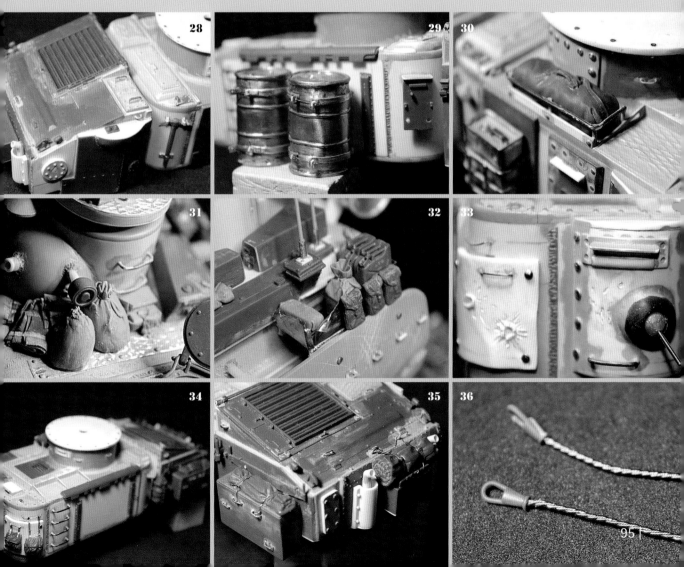

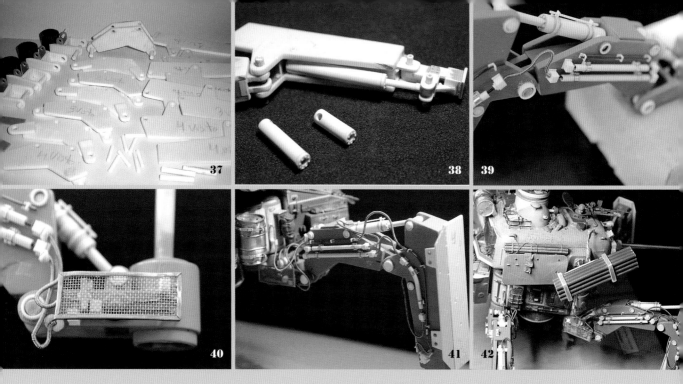

different materials in creating the rounded 3mm elevations, making these from both balsa wood and *Fórex* (*Fórex* seemed the better choice). For the covers I experimented with both *Fórex* and *Plasticard* (*Plasticard* won).

I began covering the sides with several pieces of *type 89 Trumpeter* kit [21-22]. Over these I placed other elements. On top of the body front I made a structure (from PVC and *Plasticard*) similar to that seen on the *Soviet KV* so that I could continue adding elements. Onto this base I added several cut grilles from a *type 89* kit, plus a peephole for the driver and rivets, etc.

I imagined the engine block to be a removable element that the crew could replace in the battlefield very quickly. The *Fórex* structure was covered with pieces of *type 89* kit and *Plasticard* [23-26].

Over the *type 89* kit pieces and *Plasticard* detailing I placed rivets, handles, mooring rings, boxes, banners, etc. The engine exhausts [27] are German style, simply because I liked that aesthetic, and the engine exhausts were created using *Plasticard*. The fuel can located on the right side of the body is made of tin sheet.

At the bottom of the body I also added some pieces of *89 Trumpeter* kit, rivets and further detailing. Although all these parts are located at the bottom, you can see their profiles when looking from the side, adding a sense of detail to the piece.

On the left side I attached two fuel drums [29] made from tin sheet using as a template a drum from a *Tamiya T-55* kit. When making drums from tin sheet it is very easy to create very realistic

dents simply by applying pressure with any tool.

The blankets and supplies that are distributed throughout the vehicle [30-32] are from a *Tamiya Allied Vehicles Accessories Set* which I had at home. Others were made with *Citadel* putty.

On the front of the body sits a semicircular structure to house a machine gun and a peephole for the gunner. The gun is a piece of hypodermic needle anchored to a plastic sphere that can turn within a further sphere. On both sides of the curved corners I positioned two additional shielding plates, attached to the body by bolts, which in this case were made from pins. I simulated weapons fire damage to these by heating a metal punch and pressing it into the plastic. Once a central depression is made, you can create shallow scoring radiating out from it [33].

Tow (or elevation) cables were made in two steps. First I created three cables using four copper wires for each one. I then coiled the cables into just one cable to obtain the definitive tow cable. Using this method you can create a very good approximation of reality [36].

Legs and hydraulics system

The main structure of the legs is made of plastic from a picture frame (about 3mm thick) plus PVC and *Evergreen* sheets and PVC pipes [37].

For the rotation points I made holes of 5mm diameter, which house bolts made from solid plastic rods of the same diameter.

With this basic structure tested and approved I began to add basic details: small profiles, brackets and weld lines. After checking for any imperfections I detailed the hydraulics [38-40].

The leg shields are made of *Evergreen*, marking the welds of the plates and applying some impact scoring. One of the shields is depicted as having been repaired after being almost completely destroyed, this being achieved at painting stage by going with a theme of bare metal, rust and the white markings typical of unpainted plates.

For a better alignment of bolts I placed washers in all holes, creating corresponding weld lines.

Hydraulics were made with *Evergreen* and the *Walker* was initially movable. As the leg system was fully articulated I could place the *Spider* on the diorama exactly where I wanted it. After deciding on the final pose and position I glued all the joints and hydraulics in place permanently with *Tamiya* glue.

Hydraulic hoses were made from copper wire (winding fine copper wire onto a thicker grade) glued with cyanoacrylate [41]. The connections are made from tin sheet rolled up into small tubes and the connections to the rigid pipes are small cubes of *Fórex*.

Finally I added small details such as hanging chains, rivets and bolts, beam sections welded to the legs, etc, to give a more striking appearance to the diorama. I also set about the legs making numerous scratches and scores, especially in their lower sections, as an indication of an intense operational life.

Final detailing
Final additions were many and varied, and included boxes and supplies made of putty, fabric, small logs next to the turret, locks on the shields of the turret side racks, a rifle, etc... [42].

Plastic rivets made easy
For the multitude of rivets needed in this project I tried various methods until I managed to do create them the easy way thanks to a tip explained to me by my friend Antonio Casas.

First we stretched thin plastic to the rivet diameter we wanted. Then we heated the thinned plastic with a lighter flame (without allowing the flame to actually touch the plastic) and, magically, the plastic tip became a hemisphere. Finally we cut this hemisphere flush and made another one. In this way we could create multiple rivets rapidly. We then ordered them according to size and they were ready to place on the model. [Inset opposite.]

Next time in the conclusion: Diego places the **Spider** in a super-detailed diorama.

Spider Paint Process
Due to the size of *the Spider* I had to paint areas in stages then heavily mask already painted sections [43-57].

General
Primer: *Vallejo* spray.
Rust layer: *Tamiya Rust. Vallejo Gloss Varnish* spray as protection. *Ammo Chipping Heavy Effects* prior to application of each layer.

Turret top area, body and legs
Base: *Ammo Light Green Khaki* + *Protective Green*. Lights: As previous base adding more *Ammo Light Green Khaki* and *Ochre Oil*.
Shadows: *Ammo Protective Green* + *Green Khaki* + *Russian Tank*.

White circles on the lateral turret shields
Ammo Washable White.

Turret lower area and body
Base: *AK WWI French Uniform* base + *WWI French Uniform Light*.
Lights: As previous base plus more *AK WWI French Uniform Light* and *White*.
Shadows: *AK WWI French Uniform Base* + *WWI French Uniform Shadow* + *Ammo Russian Brown*.

Rocket launcher and principal gun
Base: *Ammo Ochre Oil*.
Lights: *Ammo Ochre Oil* + *White*.
Shadows: *Ammo Ochre Oil* + *Russian Brown*.
Gloss Varnish as protection, then decals applied, then a further coat of Gloss Varnish to seal the decals.
Shading with oils.
General wash with dark brown oils.
Wash of highly diluted black oil for profiling.
Effects washes.
Rust: *AK Streaking Grime* with oils.
Grime steaks: *AK Streaking Grime*.
Dust in low areas and in horizontal areas: Airbrushed: *Tamiya Cinnamon* + *Dark Brown*. In vertical areas, dragged with a brush dipped in alcohol.

In joint recesses
Base: Gunmetal.
Washed black and dark brown oils.
Pigments on wet oil.
Pigments dry with fixative.
To bolts: *AK Oil Spill* diluted 50%. *Pigments' Clear Land*.

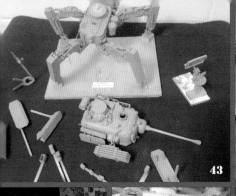

43

44

45

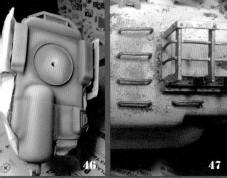

46

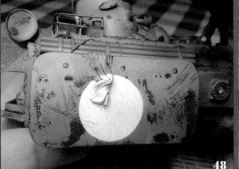

47

48

49

AK *Oil Spill* applied as grease stains. *Pigments' Clear Land* applied very smooth with excess pigment removed.

Pure steel

Base: *Ammo Chipping*.

Chipping product.

Light Grey with airbrushing in some areas.

Scratches and chipping.

Orange rust with oil-like splashes.

Chalk marks applied with a white pencil.

Graphite metallic pigment.

Hydraulics

Base: Gunmetal.

True metal *AK Iron*.

Black oil wash.

General

Black pigment at end of barrel, engine exhaust and rocket launchers.

Graphite in welds.

Grease and oil stains.

Leaves from *Mininatur*.

Snow: Bicarbonate + glue + water.

Mud on legs

Dry mud: Earth; 'balls of sea' (Seafoam? Ed.); plaster; white spirit; *AK Streaking*

Grime; dark earth pigment.

Wet mud: Earth; 'balls of sea'; plaster; white spirit; *AK Streaking Grime*; dark earth pigment; *Gloss Varnish (Humbrol)*.

Final phase.

Wet mud:

    AK Streaking Grime.

Splashes:

    AK Streaking

    Grime.

50

51

52

53

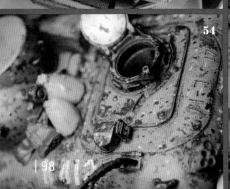

54

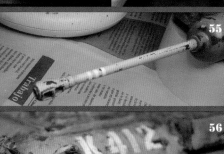

55

56

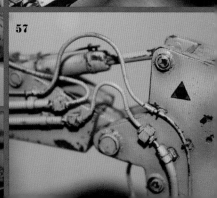

57